TAMED BY THE BEAST

INTERSTELLAR BRIDES® PROGRAM: BOOK 7

GRACE GOODWIN

GET A FREE BOOK!

JOIN MY MAILING LIST TO BE THE FIRST TO KNOW OF NEW RELEASES, FREE BOOKS, SPECIAL PRICES AND OTHER AUTHOR GIVEAWAYS.

http://freescifiromance.com

INTERSTELLAR BRIDES® PROGRAM

YOUR mate is out there. Take the test today and discover your perfect match. Are you ready for a sexy alien mate (or two)?

VOLUNTEER NOW!

interstellarbridesprogram.com

1

Tiffani Wilson, Interstellar Bride Processing Center, Earth

HE LIFTED me and my full breasts pressed into the smooth, cold surface of the wall as his cock entered me from behind. I could feel his chest looming over my back, which was a shock to my system. I was tall, just over six foot, and not one lover I'd ever had, even when I was thin, had ever been able to dominate me, manhandle me, make me feel... small. Never. Not like this.

He was massive, his presence behind me like a giant. I glanced at the huge arm that held my wrists trapped to the wall above my head. The biceps on that arm were easily the size of my thigh, and rock hard. Just like the cock stretching me open, filling me up to the brink of pain.

"Mine." The word was a barely recognizable growl but it made my pussy clamp down around him in answer. There was no doubt in his claim, only raw need, lust.

Lust? No one ever lusted for me; I was too tall, too big, too much for a man to handle. But this? *Him?*

He pushed up with a fast stroke of his hips, his hard body slamming into my mine like a conqueror. Again and again. My whole body shook with the impact, my fingers trying to gain purchase on the wall, but failing. Only his hands on my wrists, his cock deep inside me, held me up. And I loved every minute, my mind in a haze of pleasure and need, of surrender. I would give over to him. He would not relent until I did so.

Yes. I was his. I knew it somehow, knew he was mine. I had yet to see what he looked like, and I didn't care, not with his hands on my body and his hard length between my legs.

"Stay." The order was a deep rumble of sound and I looked up as he released his hold on my wrists. How had I missed him placing strange metallic bands about each of them? They were about four inches wide and carved in a beautiful pattern of gold, silver and platinum I could not focus on. His cock was clearing all thought from my mind.

With each thrust of his hips, I gasped, as if his hard length actually forced the air from my lungs.

I tried to lift my wrists, to adjust my position, but they held tight, secured by a ring embedded in the wall. Aware that it was fruitless, I tugged again and the knowledge that I couldn't move made me hotter. A sound I did not recognize as my own escaped my lips. My mate seemed to like the evidence of my submission for he growled in response and lowered his lips to the back of my neck and shoulder as he continued to pump in and out of me just fast enough to drive me wild but deny me release.

"Please." Was that me begging? God, it *was*, and I wanted to chant the word until he gave me what I craved.

In response, the man at my back, my mate, wrapped his hands around my thighs and spread me open wider, lifting me until I braced my forehead against the wall as he fucked me with a hard, pounding rhythm that drove me higher and higher, closer and closer to the edge.

The wet sound of fucking, of flesh hitting flesh filled my ears as his ragged struggle for air came from behind me.

I'd never been held like this, my legs forced apart, my pussy open and on display and completely at his mercy. The knowledge that I could do nothing but submit, nothing but accept what he gave me made me hot, so fucking hot, I'd begged him. To touch me. Bite me. Anything. Anything to push me over, to let me come.

I did not know where I was or who he truly was, but I didn't care. He was mine. My body knew that fact, accepted it, and as he lifted a hand to knead my full breast, I couldn't argue. Didn't want to.

"More." I-she-this body begged him to go harder and faster. What I really wanted, truly needed, was a hint of *more*, of pain, of intensity to break me and make me come all over his cock. It was a dark desire, one I had not yet shared aloud with anyone, but somehow he knew.

"No." His deep voice sounded more animal than man and if I knew, if I turned to look, I would not see a human behind me, but something else, something... more. The thought made me shiver with heat as I made fists and tried to use the wall as leverage to push down onto his cock, to force him to fuck me even harder. I wanted more. I wanted it all.

"More. Please." I didn't recognize my voice, but I didn't care. I sounded desperate and needy, exactly the way I felt.

He thrust hard and deep then, striking my womb and a

hint of pain shot through me. With a shudder, I threw my head back onto his shoulder and wrapped my lower legs around his thighs the best I could to hold him deep, where I needed him.

With my legs around his, he let go of my thighs to lift my breasts. With each move of his hips he shifted a nearly imperceptible amount, but the slight change of angle made his cock hit me deep over and over. He forced me to hold still, to ride him as he pinched and pulled on my nipples, tugging them to hard points until I whimpered. My pussy clenched and released his thick length and I tried to wiggle, to make him move faster.

"Mine."

Holy shit. Did he have a one-track mind! Did he need me to repeat it? Confirm it?

"Mine." Why did he keep saying that?

This body seemed to know, to understand exactly what he wanted. "Yes. Yes. Yes."

With each word he fucked me harder, as if my assent made him lose a little more control.

When he dropped one hand to rest over my clit I nearly cried with relief, but he simply held me there, no stroking, no rubbing.

The cuffs around my wrist jangled as I struggled to lift myself with my arms, to shift my hips forward and force him to touch me the way I needed.

His chuckle was so deep, that I knew, that I *felt* something so big and strong, so massive that I was truly small in comparison. And I knew he was teasing me, making me continue to beg.

"Please."

He kept one hand over my clit, the other moved up to

my hair where his large hand tangled and pulled my head back until my neck arched in a delicious offering. "Mate."

His lips grazed my ear and I shuddered at the carnal promise in that one word. Yes. I wanted him. He was mine. Forever. I licked my lips, finally ready to speak the words I knew would break his iron control. "Fuck me, mate. Make me yours."

A shudder moved through his chest and arms. I felt his whole body shake as his control shattered. He held my hair, his fierce thrusts breaking my hold on his legs as he drove in and out of me like a machine, hard, fast, unrelenting.

Pulling nearly all the way out, he used gravity to bring me back down as the weight of my own body impaled me on his cock over and over in a rapid claiming that forced a whimper from my throat.

That one sound of surrender must have been what he was waiting for as he rubbed my clit then, just a little rough, exactly the way I liked.

Head held back, I spiraled into oblivion, riding sensation after sensation as he fucked me like I was the only one for him, as if he would never get enough. As if he'd die if he didn't fill me with his seed and make me his forever.

I felt feminine and powerful. Beautiful. And I never felt beautiful. The thought distracted me until he released my hair and used his free hand to land a stinging slap on the side of my naked bottom.

I startled, my inner walls contracting around his cock. I moaned. He groaned.

He struck again, somehow knowing I loved it rough, loved the sharp tang of pain.

Smack!

Thrust. Withdraw.

Smack!

Smack!

He spanked my bottom until the heat spread like wildfire through my body, burning me up from the inside out.

When I couldn't think, could barely breathe, he stopped. Slowly, so slowly that every movement felt as if it took an eternity, he withdrew from my swollen pussy, then pushed his cock inside me once more. Fully seated, he covered my back with his sweat-slick body, caged me in, both arms wrapped around my hips, his hands eager to play with my pussy.

"Come now."

Lightly, he moved his fingers up and down above my clit, each soft strike a blast to my nerves as he spread my pussy lips open wide with two fingers of each hand and held me open to rub and flick my clit with the others. He'd been so rough and now was gentle. He could be both. He could be *everything.*

I lost hold of reality as my orgasm roared through me. In the distance, I heard a woman scream, knew it was me, but I was floating in a storm of sensation held together by my mate. I knew he had me, kept me from falling, kept me safe as I took and took and took.

My body pulsed with pleasure and I felt dizzy, disoriented for a moment. I closed my eyes and drew a shuddering breath as the spasms finally faded, as my tensed muscles relaxed. And suddenly, I felt cold, missed the heat of my mate at my back.

Panicked and unsure, I opened my eyes and blinked against the bright lights of a clinical setting. A concerned woman watched me closely from where she stood next to the strange bed on which I lay. I tried to lift my arm to rub my face, my eyes, but found I could not, my wrists cuffed to what looked like an oversized dentist's chair.

One look down at my body and reality came flooding back. A gray, hospital-style gown covered me, but was open in the back. I was naked beneath, the slide of my now wet ass and thighs testament to my body's state of arousal. I was in Miami, at the alien bride center. I'd flown here yesterday after telling my boss at the restaurant in Milwaukee to go fuck himself and walking out in the middle of my shift. That had felt fucking great.

The damn plane ticket had cost every last dime I had in the bank, but I didn't care. I needed a change. A massive change. And I wasn't going back.

"Are you all right, Miss Wilson?" The woman before me wore a dark gray uniform with a strange burgundy insignia above her left breast. I remembered her now, Warden Egara. She'd been nice enough, and completely professional, which I appreciated. Most of the time people freaked out over my size, even at the doctor's office.

The warden was trim and beautiful, and everything I'd never been. She probably had men lining up to ask her out, to get her naked and make her come all over their cocks.

Me? Men asked me to dog-sit and go get coffee. The orgasm I'd just had? Yeah, it was the first given to me by someone else since I was barely out of high school. My lovers had been few and far between, and not one of them strong enough to lift me up and fill me from behind. Or to know exactly how to touch me, how to push me to the brink, taunt me, then take me over.

I knew my eyes were glazing over, but I couldn't help relishing the memory, the feeling of that huge cock filling me up and making me a touch sore, of those huge hands making me feel beautiful and small... making me feel like... her. The other me, the me that didn't really exist, that was pure fantasy in my mind. Just like *him.*

"Miss Wilson?" The warden tilted her head down and studied me more closely, something I definitely did not need at the moment, not while my bare bottom was sliding all over the chair, wet with my own arousal.

"I'm fine." I tried to lift my hands, to adjust the hospital gown where it had inched up just past mid-thigh, but the cuffs stopped me cold. Damn.

"Are you sure? The matching process can be... intense."

So, was that what they were calling mind-numbing orgasms these days? Intense? Hell, yes, that had been intense. I'd like more then, please.

She looked sympathetic, and I found I wanted to tell her everything. Hell, I wanted to ask her the one burning question I'd been too afraid to ask. But I couldn't find the courage. I was terrified of the answer. Instead, I pasted a smile on my lips. "Yes. I'm fine."

"Excellent." She smiled and nodded, apparently convinced by my halfhearted attempt at a smile of my own that I wasn't about to go into shock or have a mental breakdown. Obviously, she'd never had to wait tables for a busy dinner shift with puking kids and drunken idiots surrounding her in equal numbers. I could handle a whole lot more stress than this. And orgasm stress? Yeah, that wasn't stress at all. It was... overwhelming.

I tried to relax, leaned back into the chair and focused on counting as I pulled air into my lungs. Four in, four out. That's how I did things.

The room was pale and white, clinical, and I felt like I was in an emergency room, not a bride processing center, but when you were about to commit to life as an alien's bride, I guess they did things a bit differently.

Her fingers moved over a small tablet too fast for me to track, and frankly, I didn't care what she was doing, as long as the stupid matching thing worked. Which, I realized, I had no idea if it had.

"Did it work? Do I have a match?" I swear my heart stopped beating as I waited for her answer.

"Oh, yes. Of course you do."

I shuddered, my sigh loud, even to my own ears, and she lifted a hand to my shoulder in a sympathetic gesture. "I'm sorry, I didn't realize you were worried about that. You've been matched to Atlan."

I didn't know a thing about Atlan, but that didn't stop hope spreading in my chest like wildfire. I'd been matched. Holy crap. "And this matching thing... you're sure that the alien will want me to be his mate? You're sure the matching works?"

"Absolutely." She patted my shoulder one more time and returned her attention to the table.

"Even for girls like me?" Shit. My deepest fear slipped past my lips before I could stop it. I bit down and hoped nothing else slipped out.

That stopped her cold and she lifted her gaze to mine. "What do you mean, girls like you? Are you married? Because that was one question you were required to answer under oath. If you lied, I can't process you."

Married? As if.

I sighed. Jeeeez. Did I have to spell it out for her? With her size-eight body and C-cup breasts, she had probably never worried about being wanted. I studied her concerned gray eyes and decided that, yes, I did have to spell it out for her. Damn it. I took a deep breath and gathered my courage, spitting out the words as fast as I could. "Girls like me. Big girls."

She raised her brows, as if surprised, her gaze raking up and down my very plus-sized body in a quick survey before returning her attention to my face. Her grin was one of the best things I'd ever seen. "Don't worry about being too small for an Atlan, dear. I know that to an Atlan warlord, you'll seem a bit undersized, but you're his matched mate. You'll be perfect for each other."

"Too small?" Was she freaking kidding me? I hadn't been able to shop off the rack since tenth grade.

"Atlan females are at least a foot taller than the average woman on Earth, and the Atlans need their females to be strong enough to tame them."

"What do you mean, tame them?"

"They are not human, Tiffani. Atlan warriors have a beast that lives within them. When they are in battle, or want to fuck, the beast comes out. Think of it as an entire planet of males like The Incredible Hulk. You might be a bit smaller than they're used to, but strength is mental as well as physical. You'll be perfect for him."

My mind wandered to the giant hand that had gripped my wrists, the huge cock stretching me open, the massive chest pressed to my back...

I shuddered in anticipation. Yes. I wanted that again. If that was what an Atlan male was like, I was game. Absolutely. "Okay. I'm ready."

She chuckled then. "Not so fast. First we have to go through some standard protocols. For the record, please state your name."

"Tiffani Wilson."

She nodded. "Are you currently, or have you ever been married?"

"No."

"Have you produced any biological offspring?"

"No."

Her fingers moved swiftly as she continued, her voice monotone and robotic, as if she'd recited the exact same words hundreds of times. "As a bride, you will never return to Earth as you've been matched to Atlan, as all travel will be determined and controlled by your new planet's laws and customs. You will surrender your citizenship of Earth and become an official citizen of your new world."

Holy crap. Her words hit me like a blast of cold air, and the enormity of my decision struck home. No longer a citizen of Earth? How was that even possible?

I felt cold, hard panic creep up my spine with icy fingers as the wall to my left shifted, opening to reveal a small enclosure lit with bright blue light.

"Um..."

"Your bride fee will be donated to the Wisconsin Humane Society Milwaukee, is that correct?" she asked, as if she could not sense my growing concern. No longer a citizen of Earth? I wanted a mate, but maybe I'd gone too far.

"Miss Wilson?"

"Yes, donate the fee." I didn't need the money since I would *no longer be a citizen of Earth*, and I had no one I cared about to give it to. I lost my fifteen-year-old calico, Sofie, last year to leukemia. My parents were both dead, my cousins lived across the country in California and we were far from close. I was alone in the world with nothing to lose.

My chair slid sideways and a large, metallic arm came toward me from where it was anchored in the wall with what looked like a giant needle on its end. I leaned side-ways, trying to avoid it.

"Don't worry, Tiffani. That's just going to install your NPU."

"What the hell is that?" I eyed the needle with a very large sense of trepidation.

"Neural Processing Unit. It will help you learn and understand the Atlan language."

Okay. I held still and clenched my hands so tightly my knuckles turned white. So, a *Star Trek*-style universal trans-lator thing? Whatever.

The needle punctured my skin, just behind my temple and I bit down, trying to ignore the pain as the device swiftly withdrew, rotated to my left, and repeated the process on the other side.

When it moved back to its place, nestled in the wall, my chair lurched and I began to sink into a warm pool of clear, blue water.

"'Your processing will begin in three, two..."

I closed my eyes. Adrenaline made my heart pound as I waited for her to say, "one." Waited, and waited.

She sighed. "Not again."

My chair stopped moving and I opened my eyes to see her frowning. She hurried to a panel on the wall in the exam room as I watched.

My eyes widened in fear and confusion. "What's wrong?"

She glanced at me quickly, then away, not making eye contact. "There's a problem at the Atlan transport center. I'm sorry. This has only happened once before."

Great. They didn't want me. I knew it, could feel it deep down. My heart imploded in my chest, all the hope I'd just given free rein, hope that I'd finally find a man who actually *wanted* me, who thought me beautiful and sexy and desirable? Gone, and the remnants were sharp blades in my gut, made worse because I'd dared to hope for something different. "Fine. Get me out of this chair so I can go home."

She shook her head, ignoring me as she spoke to someone on the screen, someone I couldn't see. I could hear the voice coming through. It was a woman's voice, but I couldn't make out her words, only the warden's.

"What's going on, Sarah?" She paused, listened. "What? But that's impossible." Another pause. "I see. So, what does Warlord Dax want me to do about it?" I heard the growing agitation in her voice. "No, he has a mate, and she's human. She's strapped to the chair right now, ready for processing." A long delay. "I can't. The transport permissions have been automatically deactivated by the system. I'll need new ones." She sighed. "Okay. Give me five minutes."

The warden said goodbye and walked toward me with her brows drawn together, her lips in a thin line. Her shoulders were tight and her steps were short and clipped, as if her muscles were so tense she could barely move.

"What's wrong? Tell me what's happening." I strained against the cuffs as the warden raised her hand in a motion meant to pacify me.

"Your mate, Commander Deek, has been lost to mating fever."

That was not what I'd expected. I assumed she'd say that my mate had changed his mind. But mating fever? "What does that mean?"

She sighed and dropped her hand to her side. "Atlan warriors are very big; they're the largest, strongest warriors in the entire Coalition Fleet."

My pussy clenched at her words. Oh, hell yeah, I knew exactly how big they were. "So?"

"So, as I explained, they also possess the ability to go into what they refer to as beast mode, becoming larger and stronger in the heat of battle, or when they are..."

"Fucking?" The deep rumbling growl in my ear from the processing dream, the monosyllabic conversation, made more and more sense now. Beast mode. Damn, that was hot. "So? They're like the Hulk when he's angry. Got it. You already told me that. What's the problem?"

"If they wait too long to claim a mate, they lose control of their beast side. They transform and can't restrain themselves. They've been known to kill their own friends and allies, men they've fought beside for years. At that point no one else can save them. They only recognize and respond to one person in the entire universe."

I waited, barely able to breathe as she finished.

"Their mate."

I relaxed, the tension draining from my shoulders. "Okay. Great. Send me to him now. That's what the protocol says, right? If he only recognizes his mate, he'll know me and get his beast under control."

She shook her head. "It's not that simple. Atlans are linked to their mates through special binding cuffs."

I remembered the beautiful golden cuffs around my wrists, the strange designs. "So, I need a pair of cuffs in order to help him?"

"You have to already be bonded to him, to already be his mate, in order to control his beast. I'm afraid he's lost."

"Lost? They can't find him?"

"No, the beast has taken over. I'm so sorry, Tiffani, but he's beyond saving."

Beyond saving? The one man in the universe who was supposed to be perfect for me, supposed to want me and love me and accept me, beyond saving? "Then what happens to him?"

At last, she met my gaze, and I wished she hadn't. All I saw in her eyes was a deep, dark well of pity and pain. "My contact on Atlan, a bride I sent not long ago, says he's scheduled for execution."

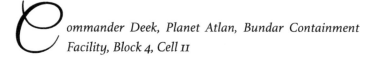

ommander Deek, Planet Atlan, Bundar Containment Facility, Block 4, Cell 11

I STARTLED AWAKE, my body slick with sweat. The cot beneath me was too small for my frame in beast mode and I shifted onto my side. Three days. I'd been in this hell for three days. When I'd witnessed Dax's fever come upon him, it had come upon him over two weeks, slowly building. But it had been in the height of battle and his rages had been disguised at first as battle adrenaline. Understandable, considering what the warlord had witnessed and fought against.

Most Atlan warriors had their fever build slowly, allowing them time to find their mate before their inner beast took over. But I wasn't a normal Atlan warrior, it seemed, for I'd gone from a battle commander to a beast condemned within a day.

I'd raged through *Battleship Brekk* and it had taken four

warriors to pin me down. Warlord Engel, visiting from Atlan, and no doubt eager to press the issue of his unmated daughter upon me once more, had been present when I lost control, had witnessed me attacking a young Prillon warrior during my rage. I could not recall that incident, for I was too far gone with the fever, but I'd wreaked havoc on the ship. A planned attack on a nearby Hive outpost had to be postponed and the sector gain we'd made against the enemy had been reversed. In the med unit, I'd been diagnosed with Phase Three Beast Complex. It was the final phase of a warrior's deterioration. The phase where my mind would regain control less and less often, until I went full Beast and never came back.

There was no cure except a mating bond. I'd have to fuck my mate while in beast mode, coming deep inside her, marking her, claiming her and making her mine. Fucking in beast mode was not an issue. I could feel him within, his rage building and seeking an outlet for release. But I faced no Hive soldiers to kill, and I had no mate.

None. I was a threat to safety if I failed to take a mate, for even now, my fever did not wane. Simply lying in the cool cell, without battle or a female nearby to provoke the beast, the monster within me raged. Sweat soaked my skin, my clothes. Basic restraints had done nothing to contain me. I'd ripped them from the wall within the first five minutes of my confinement. Only the graviton force field was strong enough to hold a beast, and my cell had that powerful energy field hidden within every wall, the ceiling and the floor. The front of the cell appeared to be nothing but empty air, but I knew differently, had thrown myself against the grav-wall time and again while in beast mode last night. My strength could not defeat it. My beast had tried, but lost.

And so, immediately after transport back to my home world, back to Atlan, I'd been summarily sentenced to execution. Dax had visited and had afforded me four days' delay, hoping that the fever would diminish or a mate would appear.

The way I felt, constantly on edge, my beast prowling inside me, ready to attack anything that came within reach, I knew the fever would not end. I would be forced to fuck. But the female before me now did not incite lust, but anger.

I growled, letting it rumble through my body at the futility of it all. How had this come about? I was of an age for the fever, yes, but not like this! There were no signs, no history with the males in my family line of losing control like I had.

My father died in the Hive wars when I was still a boy, but he fought for many years and died with honor. My grandfather fought for nearly a decade and come home, took a mate and still served on the other side of the planet as an advisor to top council members. None of my cousins had ever succumbed to the fever. The fact that I had, made me a blight on the family name.

And I still didn't understand what had happened.

The nearly uncontrollable rage had come on so unexpectedly and intensely that I lost focus, my mind solely on soothing the beast. I could not think clearly, could not speak coherently or with any logic to defend myself or my death sentence after I attacked the Prillon warrior. My beast, restless and edgy my entire life, had become wild and inconsolable.

For the first time in my life, I was out of control. And I did not like the feeling.

The only avenue left to me was a mate. Somehow, the

Atlan females who walked past my cell did nothing for my beast. Unmated themselves, they volunteered to soothe the beasts within the warriors who were locked up, their last chance to mate and end the fever. It worked frequently, but the beast within the warrior had to be receptive, had to *want* the female. Fucking for release with a female that was appealing enough was well and good for an Atlan male, but not enough during mating fever.

Only taking a mate would do. The warrior in the cell to the left of mine had found a worthy mate, for I could hear the rough sounds of fucking. Wild cries of pleasure, wet slaps of skin against skin, and the growls of the beast were loud in the cavernous corridors. This cellblock was nearly empty, just three of us locked up, and all from wealthy, highly respected families.

While my cock pulsed and throbbed, I tore open the front of my pants and stroked the thick length, trying to ease the discomfort. The sounds of fucking helped me stroke my cock to release, thinking of a mate beneath me, spread open for my cock, eager to have me take her hard and make her mine. I could see her cuffs about her wrists, the connection that was formed when my seed spilled inside her. But I could not see her face. And when my seed spurted over my hand and onto the floor, the fever did not taper. Nor did my need for the faceless mate that I knew would not—could not—save me.

Ripping my shirt over my head, I used it to wipe the seed from my fingers, dropped it onto the floor and put my foot on it to wipe up the spilled pool. Tucking my still erect cock back into my pants, I took a deep breath, then another.

The fire in my blood, the wild rage did not lessen its hold. Fuck. If I couldn't get past this, I was going to be executed. And maybe that was a good thing. My beast was a fury in my head, a wild animal clawing at its cage, willing to die to be free.

"You look... well, Commander."

My head whipped about at the apprehensive greeting. He was right to be afraid. Beyond the grav-wall stood Warlord Engel Steen and his daughter, the Atlan beauty I'd been expected I mate from the age of five, the stunning Tia. My beast had yet to find interest in her and I had long ago assumed it was not a match. They both looked at me as if I were an exotic animal in a zoo. Perhaps I was one, trapped behind the grav-wall and ogled by strangers, constantly under surveillance. The sound of a mating bond being formed continued from the next cell and Tia's cheeks turned an embarrassed shade of pink, her arousal scenting the air as I watched her, inspected her yellow gown and the swell of her ample breasts, hoping my beast would calm, would show the smallest interest in a female.

In the nearby cell, the newly mated female screamed her release as the warrior in beast mode growled. When the growling ceased, I knew that warrior's fever had been instantly soothed. He would walk out of his cell soon, soothed and mated. A free warrior once again.

I didn't care that the Atlan had fucked a willing female, felt her lush body beneath his, enjoyed the hot, wet heat of her pussy, but I was damn jealous that the beast within him was finally appeased. It seemed nothing would please mine. He pushed at my control every moment of every day, as if he were already rabid, beyond saving. And even now, with a willing female standing before him, he prowled the cage of my mind, unsatisfied with what she offered. My logical mind knew I should take what had been offered dozens of times, throw Tia up against the wall and fuck her, allow her to cuff me and do her best to control me when the beast raged against the restraints.

But even as I thought of the possibility, my beast growled a warning. He was not interested. He would not acknowledge this woman as his mate, would not be tamed by her presence.

"That could be you," Engel said, tilting his head toward the other cell, then looking down at Tia with an obvious question in his raised brows. A question I could not answer. The beast chose the mate, not I, and it did not want Tia. Fucking her would not change that. For years I'd laughed at the absurd claim of other warriors I knew who'd tried to explain this fact to me. I'd ignored them, at my peril. The beast was in charge now. All I could do was sit back and thank the gods he'd allowed me control long enough to get rid of our visitors.

Tia took a step closer to the grav-wall and the scent of her bathing oil, spices and nerdera flower, enveloped me as the air filtration system pumped their combined scents into the cell.

Revulsion made my beast growl. No. I had known her my entire life, and we both knew I held no desire for her. I admired and respected her, but my feelings were similar to those I held for my sister. My beast refused to become aroused by her. In fact, he became angrier each time they appeared with the same words, the same enticements. Engel wanted me to mate his daughter. My beast would not accept her. I'd told the man many, many times.

"We've come to offer you a second chance," he continued. "You will be executed in three days, Commander. Surely, we would all prefer to avoid that."

"Second chance?" I said, my voice rough and deep, so unfamiliar to me. It was more like twentieth, but I held my tongue.

"You don't remember?" Tia asked, her gaze fixated on my bare chest. I could not miss her interest or her arousal at the sight of my body. In fact, I could smell the wet welcome of her pussy, but my beast skulked, refusing to be tempted.

She was a tall woman, statuesque. The perfect example of an Atlan bride. Her dark hair flowed long and free down her back and her floor-length yellow gown, the crisscross of gold outlining her perfect breasts showed off both her status as a wealthy Atlan elite, and her dark coloring to perfection. She was extremely beautiful, but my beast didn't want anything to do with her. It would be so much fucking easier if he did.

Afraid to speak, worried my beast would snap or snarl, I shook my head.

"Your beast gains more control each day, Commander. We came yesterday. Tia offers herself to you as a mate. Let her save you."

"She should speak for herself then." I couldn't hold the words back, for Engel wouldn't have escorted her if he did not have his own machinations. I just didn't know what they were. As a member of the ruling class, he had been in charge of interplanetary shipments and supplies for more than a decade. He was a very powerful man, wealthy and well connected, a ten-year veteran of the Hive wars. Engel wouldn't come here to pawn off his daughter, to stand by as a beast fucked her, just to get her mated. She had her choice of mates.

"Why me?"

Tia's cheeks blushed red and she bit her plump lower lip

in a move practiced and well perfected. I knew. I'd watched her tempt warriors with that look many times before I'd joined the Coalition Fleet. "I'm willing, Deek. You know I've cared for you since I was a girl. We have known each other for years, and I wish for this union. I find you... attractive. We could be good together."

Tia's admittance surprised me, and my beast. While she may have been interested, my beast had never once found significance in her. I knew the beast's desire would flare to life when I found the right mate, yet I never had. I'd fucked females, plenty of them, but Tia didn't want just a hard fuck with a condemned warrior. She wanted to mate me. She wanted forever. She wanted me to give her control of my beast.

"Why me, Tia?"

"You were my best friend. It's always been you, ever since we were young ones in the nursery. You know I followed you around like a shadow. Always. I don't want to see you die, Deek. Please. I want to spend the rest of my life by your side, as your mate."

My beast roared to life. "No," it shouted, pushing to the fore. My skin tightened and the heat of the beast roared through my veins. The muscles bulged on my neck and arms and my back elongated, stretching to accommodate the monster straining to break free. I pushed him back, barely holding on to control as Tia gasped, backing away from the grav-wall.

"Then you die," Engel said, his gaze narrowed and filled with a level of hatred I'd never seen from him before. It was not my intention to hurt Tia, but the beast was in control, and the beast was tired of having the same female be thrown at him over and over, despite his rejections.

I breathed hard, tried to calm my pounding heart so I could respond. "I would take her here, fuck her against the wall. I would not be gentle. I would hurt her, Engel; her presence does not calm my rage. You want that for Tia?" I asked him, my hands clenched into fists.

Tia put a hand on her father's shoulder. "Let me speak with him, Father."

Engel nodded, gave me a hard look, then left.

Tia remained. She walked to the side of the grav-wall and removed a small black pouch from her pocket, placing it in the slot used to pass items to me without the risk of lowering the grav-walls protective shield. She pressed a button and the small drawer slid through the wall to emerge on my side of the containment cell.

I opened the hatch and looked down to see my great-grandmother's most beloved possession, a family heirloom that had been passed to Tia's family line three generations ago. I knew what was inside the engraved pouch, but still, I could not resist opening the top and pouring the wealth of gold links into my hand.

I looked at it, then at her. "Why would you give this to me?"

"You are afraid you are too rough for me, that the beast within you will hurt me. It is a present, for the beast. Perhaps touching something that has touched my skin will ease your fever in some small way."

I lifted the necklace from my palm. The small elaborate gold and graphite coils were cool to the touch, smooth. If the gift was meant to pacify me, it was not working. Nothing would work from Tia, for she was not my mate. My life would be so much easier if my beast would accept her. But he refused.

I placed the necklace back into its pouch and sent it back to Tia using the small drawer. "Keep it, Tia. When you find the mate you are destined for, neither the necklace nor your eagerness will be denied."

"Please, Deek. At least try..." She lifted a hand to her shoulder and shrugged her gown off the side, exposing her entire shoulder, her neck and most of her breast.

"No." My voice rose as I spoke, the beast was eager to tell her off. She was not my mate, and the beast was eager to ensure she would not return. I had no desire to waste the short time I had left giving her false hope. "We were friends as children, Tia. But I've been gone a long time. I am not the same man that left. And as much as I wish you were, you are not my mate. The beast can smell your desire, the wet heat of your pussy. He does not desire you. We will not allow me to touch you. I am sorry."

Anger flared in her eyes as she tilted her chin up and I saw a flash of the childhood hellion I remembered so well. "You are so stubborn, Deek! Tell your beast to shut up and accept what is offered."

"I can't. It doesn't work that way."

"Why not? You'd rather die?"

"It's not my choice. The beast is in control now. If my true mate is not found, if she can't soothe the mating fever, if my beast will not surrender to her, then yes, I die willingly. I cannot live with this fever raging in my blood."

I was prepared for death, expected it even. Tia's shocked expression surprised me. Why should my honesty distress her? Was she expecting me to change my mind and take her out of desperation? The beast would not allow that to occur. The beast would rather die, and probably would. Warlord Engel was right about one thing... I was running out of time.

She pursed her lips as if she would say more, but she didn't. She retrieved the necklace and watched me for a minute that felt like an eternity.

"Goodbye, Deek. I hope you find what you're looking for. And if you change your mind, I've left my information with the guards."

"Thank you, Tia. But I won't change my mind."

She nodded. Turning on her heel, she readjusted her dress to cover herself and walked out of sight. I knew she would not return.

What logic I had left wondered if she was truly my last chance at survival?

The beast within said no. He didn't want her. Didn't like anything about her. It never had.

And yet, the beast still raged, still demanded his mate.

I dropped down onto the bed, my head in my hands. The beast pressed at my mind like a tidal wave rushing toward the shore to wipe out what remained of my sanity.

My mate would not come, and I would die.

Tiffani

"Execution?" I pulled on the restraints that held me to the table in the processing room in a futile act of panic. "No. They can't kill him."

Warden Egara's smile was sad. "I'm afraid that is the Atlan way. Once a male is lost to the mating fever, there is no redemption."

"But he has a mate! Me! I can redeem him, save him.

Whatever," I pleaded with her. There had to be some kind of mistake. This couldn't be happening. I had a guy who wanted me and he was set to be executed? I think not. "Send me there. The protocol matched us. Officially, by alien law, he's mine. Isn't that correct? I am already his mate. Doesn't that grant me some kind of rights? I have the right to see him. I demand to see him."

Her eyebrows lifted into severe arcs as she considered me long and hard. She looked over her shoulder and spoke. "Can you hear her, Sarah?" The warden nodded her head, listening. She was having a conversation with someone on the far side of the universe. If I wasn't in a processing center, I'd think she was crazy. Especially since *I* couldn't understand a thing the woman was saying. Her voice was too faint, and all I could hear was the pounding of my rage in my ears. "And what if something goes wrong?"

A deep, rumbling voice came through the speaker then, much louder and more commanding. It reminded me of the voice from my vision and a shiver of rekindled need raced across my skin. "There's no room for mistakes. If she comes to us, she must have the courage to see it through. Should she fail, he dies," the voice boomed, startling me.

Warden Egara turned to me and I hardened my resolve. No one, and I mean no one, was stealing this from me. "I won't fail. He's mine."

The warden nodded, turning back to the screen, to the large Atlan male I could hear but not see. "I believe her, Warlord. I think we should give her a chance to save him."

"Very well. I'm not prepared to give up on the commander. Send her to us. We will get her in to see him."

Warden Egara actually bowed her head before responding, as if she were speaking to royalty or something. "As you wish, Warlord Dax. If you have transport codes, I will initiate her transport now."

"They should be arriving at any moment."

Even as he spoke, the bright blue lights behind me began to flash and brighten and my chair jerked into motion. "What's happening?"

"Received. Thank you. The commander's mate is on her way." Warden Egara ended her call and walked toward me with a sad smile on her face. "Good luck, Tiffani. I am sending you to Warlord Dax and his mate, Sarah. She is from Earth and recently matched. They will help you break in to see your mate."

That didn't sound good. Unlawful. Dangerous.

"Break in? Why would I have to break in?"

"He's in Atlan prison, dear. On death row, as we call it. And you are not an Atlan female, or a member of his family."

That made no sense. He'd committed no crime other than having his own genetic nature take its course. But I would be committing a crime to see him? I was the one who would be breaking the laws?

"But I'm his mate. And you said I would be a citizen of Atlan now, no longer a citizen of Earth. I should be allowed to see him. I shouldn't have to break in anywhere."

She nodded. "Very true, but rules are rules. And only Atlan females are allowed into the containment facilities. Good luck. I hope your attempts are enough to save you both." She checked her tablet once more and I had a flash of déjà vu as she lifted her head and spoke. "When you wake, you will be on Atlan. Your processing will begin in three... two..."

I tensed, waiting for that last word and wondering what

the hell I had just gotten myself into. Breaking into prison? Death row? Beast mode? Holy shit.

"One."

The blue light flashed and I sank deeper into the pale blue water. I felt like I was inside an egg as the door to the examination room slid closed, locking me within. I closed my eyes and waited, terrified of what would happen next, but the longer I was in the water, the more relaxed I felt.

Were they freaking drugging me? The idea of breaking in to a prison didn't seem quite so bad. Nor did a mate who was part beast. I felt... relaxed.

When my eyelids drifted closed with an irresistible urge to sleep I realized, yes, they absolutely were pumping me full of some kind of feel-good, either in the water or in the air, and I simply didn't care.

Tiffani, Planet Atlan, Warlord Dax's Fortress

I AWOKE on a soft bed that made my king-sized mattress at home look like a twin. A fabric as soft as silk cushioned my cheek and I stroked the soft, cream-colored fabric as I looked around the room. I had landed in the middle of a freaking fairytale castle. The room was larger than my one-bedroom apartment back home, the walls looked like pale blue and gray marble. Plush rugs with scenes of oddly colored birds and trees littered the floor and a huge canopy draped the bed, making me feel like I was in a secret clubhouse.

Elaborate designs decorated white crown molding with swirls of gold and pewter gray that looked strangely similar to the cuffs I'd worn in my dream. And everything, from the couch and chair across the room, to the pillows, was bigger than I'd ever seen before. I wondered just how big these

Atlan warriors truly were. And how big were their women? A human child would need a small ladder to get up on that couch.

"You're awake." The voice was friendly, female and spoke in English. I rolled over to see a petite brunette smiling at me. She was dressed like a princess in a flowing green-and-gold gown, her hair piled on top of her head in an elaborate up-do I could never hope to master. Her eyes were a warm brown, and full of sympathy as they looked at me. "How's your head? Those NPUs can be brutal for the first few days."

"NPU?" I blinked and tried to sit. With the movement, a flash of pain, like an icepick in my temple, made me groan.

"Yep, that's what I thought." She grinned and leaned forward with a glowing blue stick of some sort, which she waved around near my face. "Hold still. The ReGen wand will help with the headache."

"Thanks." I held still, but my eyes followed the wand back and forth, wondering what the hell she was doing. But it seemed to help and the headache faded. With it went the nausea. And a few moments later, blessedly, the room stopped spinning. I needed one of those.

"The NPU is a translator. While I obviously speak English, the Atlans don't. It allows you to understand all languages. Better?" she asked.

I nodded and I didn't feel a hint of pain.

She pulled the ReGen wand back and turned if off somehow, setting it on a decorative, gold-flecked nightstand next to the bed before holding out her right hand. "I'm Sarah."

"Tiffani."

"Nice to meet you." She shook my hand, her grip warm

but firm and I noticed the elegantly carved gold bands on her wrists.

"So, you're mated to an Atlan, too?"

Her smile was a mile wide and gave me hope. "Yep. Dax is all mine. We had a rough start, but I love it here. So tell me, how's Earth?"

It seemed an odd question, but I wasn't actually on Earth anymore. "Um, well, the same, I guess."

"Where are you from?"

"Wisconsin."

Sarah nodded. "I was an Army brat. I moved so much, nowhere ever really felt like home. I miss Earth, but I don't. I belong here, and soon you will, too."

I scooted to the edge of the bed and looked down at my body. I was dressed in a gown similar to the one Sarah wore, but instead of green and gold, it was a deep burgundy that I knew would bring out the red highlights in my hair. It fit me perfectly, and I had to wonder where they'd gotten the darn thing. It wasn't like I could buy clothes off the rack at home and I definitely hadn't gone clothes shopping on Atlan while I slept. Unlike Sarah, my wrists were bare.

She must have read my mind. "Oh, isn't that color perfect? It brings out your eyes."

"Yes. I... thank you. But where did you get it?"

She rose to her feet and began to pace beside the bed. Back and forth, making me nervous once more. "Don't worry. We borrowed it from Deek's sister. She's about your size, which is small for an Atlan, but it will have to do until we can get a seamstress here to fit you."

Small for an Atlan? So, Warden Egara hadn't been kidding.

I scooted to the edge and stood, trying to get a feel for

having my legs beneath me. The dress was actually a bit too large, but very flattering. It hugged my large breasts, a band of gold crisscrossing in the front and boosting them from below. I'd seen something similar in television shows of ancient Romans or Greeks in togas. "They dress like ancient Greek gods?"

Sarah burst out laughing as I inspected my gown. "Just the women. Wait until you see these boys in their armor. Hubba-hubba, baby." She waggled her eyebrows. "You won't be able to keep your hands off your man."

That sounded good to me, but it made me remember my purpose. "Speaking of my mate, Warden Egara said he's scheduled to be executed."

That stopped Sarah in her tracks and she turned to me. "Yes. You don't have much time to save him. He's to be executed in three days if he doesn't take a mate and prove he can control his beast. Dax is beside himself as they're good friends. They fought together in the Hive war for a long time. He's probably pacing right now. We've been waiting forever for you to wake up."

"How long was I out?"

"Half a day. The time is pretty similar here. Their days last twenty-six hours, but I was always a night owl, so the longer days don't bother me."

"Okay." I didn't really care about that right now, but I filed it away for later. I had three days—and a generous two extra hours for each one—to save my mate and control his beast. I wasn't exactly sure how I was going to do that, but I was willing to do anything. The Atlan warrior was mine and I wasn't going to let anything happen to him. "Let's go. Warden Egara said you would help me get in to see him."

Sarah walked to the door and opened it. I followed

behind her, exiting the luxurious bedroom for a long hallway that looked like a royal decorator had been given unlimited access to cash. I wasn't familiar with the artifacts that lined the hallway, the vases and carved tables, the painted murals and fresh flowers everywhere, in every imaginable color. I didn't know what they called this stuff, but I recognized money when I saw it.

I cleared my throat. "So, are you a princess or what? I feel like I'm in Cinderella's castle."

That made her laugh. "Yes. Dax is a celebrated warlord. When the Atlan men return from the war, they are treated like kings. We have another castle in the northern lands that I haven't even seen yet, and more land, titles and money than I can even comprehend."

If we'd been on Earth and spoke like that, I'd think she was gloating, but she didn't seem the type.

Shock registered in my system after a moment. I knew a lot of veterans who came home from fighting broke and without a place to stay. "How can they afford to do that for all their vets? That's amazing."

Sarah looked over her shoulder at me, sadness in her eyes, and opened another door. "Not that many make it back. They are on the front lines with the Hive, on the ground. I know what it's like. I've been there, fought for the Coalition myself. They fight like demons, but either they get taken down in battle, or they lose control of their beast. The ones who come home are the strongest warriors, and they are treated like gods."

I grinned. "So, you're mated to a god?"

Her smile was pure wicked. "Yes. And so are you."

She held the door open and I preceded her into a long dining room with a table that would seat at least thirty. The chairs were high-backed black wood of some sort I'd never seen before. Seated at the head of the table was a giant.

He stood, and I stopped in my tracks. Holy shit, he was big. Well over seven feet tall with shoulders twice the width of mine. He was dressed in form-fitting black armor that hugged every damn muscle, from ripped abs to rock-hard thighs and I knew my jaw dropped, but I couldn't seem to close it.

Sarah closed the door behind us and walked around to step into her mate's waiting arms. She was probably five eight, and she looked almost childlike next to him.

"Welcome to our home, Tiffani. I am Warlord Dax."

His deep voice rumbled through me and I would have stepped backward, but Sarah had her hands wrapped around his waist like he was just a big teddy bear. While I feared he could crush me with just a tight grip, I had to give him the benefit of the doubt. His words were not spoken in English, but even as the thought passed through my mind, the strange processor they'd implanted in my skull translated the words directly into my head, like a thought. Amazing. "I'm Tiffani Wilson. Nice to meet you."

He indicated I should take a seat, but I was too nervous. I wanted to go see my mate. He was the reason I was here, and since the moment Sarah had told me he only had three days left, it was as if I had a ticking time bomb in the back of my mind. Three days was not a lot of time.

On the table in front of him were four golden bands, two similar to the ones on Sarah's wrists, and two much larger. I glanced at Warlord Dax and confirmed my suspicions. He wore cuffs nearly identical to Sarah's, only bigger.

He noticed my attention. "Commander Deek's sister

brought these for you when she brought the dress. They are carved with the markings of Deek's house."

"His name is Deek?" I asked. It was the first time I heard it and I wanted to know more.

"Yes, he is an Atlan ground commander from *Battleship Brekk*. He served for ten years, and I with him. He saved my life more than once, and I would not see him die now."

Impressive. It only intrigued me further.

I walked to the table and picked up the nearest cuff. Dark, pewter-colored swirls created a complex design in the heavy gold. Beneath that, so small as to be nearly impossible to see with the naked eye, I saw computer circuitry of some sort. Confused, I lifted my gaze to find both Sarah and Dax watching me.

"I thought these were like wedding rings or something. But they are full of computer circuits. What, exactly, do they do?"

Sarah spoke first. "Once you are both wearing them, they will bind you to the commander. You will not be able to be more than a short distance from him without feeling extreme physical pain."

"What?" That was totally bogus. "Like a leash?"

Sarah rolled her eyes. "There is no tether, but trust me, you will stay near. If you get too far from his side, it's like taking a shot from a Taser."

I opened my mouth to protest, but Warlord Dax interrupted me.

"It will be the same for him, Tiffani. The close proximity of our mate can be the only thing that keeps our beast under control. It soothes us to know our mate is nearby. Once you are truly mated and he has overcome the mating fever, you may choose to wear the cuffs or not. But in the beginning, they serve as protection. If you can get them on his wrists, they are the best chance you will have at saving his life."

Without taking a moment to consider, I lifted the smaller cuff to my wrist and closed it, a sense of finality settling on my shoulders as it sealed itself. There was no seam, making it impossible for me to find a way to remove it.

Too late for second thoughts. I came halfway across the galaxy to save my mate. I wasn't going to let a pair of cuffs stop me. I locked the second cuff around my opposite wrist and grabbed the larger pair, held them up. "Okay. How do I get these on him?"

Warlord Dax took a deep breath. "Very carefully."

I nodded. "Okay. Let's do this. I'm ready."

Sarah disappeared for a moment and returned with a large hooded cloak. "Here, wear this."

I slid the heavy burgundy cloak over my shoulders, pulled the two sides together in front of me. She nodded her head vigorously. "Good. Now pull up the hood."

I pulled the hood forward and it eclipsed my face by nearly six inches.

Warlord Dax touched my shoulder. "Excellent. Keep the cuffs hidden until you are inside. And whatever you do, don't look at anyone, and don't remove the cloak until we give you the signal."

"What's the signal?"

Sarah was practically dancing with excitement. "Dax has a friend on the inside. He served under the commander as well. He's going to shut down the surveillance system inside Deek's cell so you two can be alone."

"We're going to stay inside the prison cell?" That had

never been one of my thoughts. When Warden Egara mentioned breaking in, I assumed it meant breaking my mate out as well.

Sarah nodded.

"Come. It is time." Warlord Dax moved swiftly out of the room as I struggled to hold the large cuffs somewhere no one would see them.

Sarah stepped up, took the cuffs from my hands, and showed me where the pockets were, hiding them instantly in the deep folds of the cloak. "Listen, Dax doesn't feel comfortable talking about this in front of you, but if you want to save Deek, you're going to have to be willing to do whatever it takes."

That was the reason I was here. "I came halfway across the galaxy to claim a man on death row. I think I've proved I'm willing to do whatever it takes."

Sarah's hand landed on my shoulder and she peered up at me beneath the hood of my cloak. "Good. Because you've got to get these cuffs on him so he can be connected with you, so his beast can sense you and begin to settle. And the only way you're going to do that is to get really damn close."

I bit my lip. "Will he hurt me?"

Sarah shook her head. "I don't know. Under normal circumstances, no way. No Atlan warrior would ever hurt a female. But if he's in the middle of an attack of mating fever, I don't know what he'll do."

"So, how am I supposed to calm him down?"

Her grin was contagious, and I would have smiled back if I weren't totally freaking out. "Fuck his brains out. Give yourself to him and let his beast fuck you until he is satisfied, then slam the cuffs on his wrists when he's not expecting it. Don't worry, his beast should recognize you as his mate, cuffs or not."

My eyebrows rose at her words, at the very vivid and carnal task, but Dax yelled at us to hurry. Sarah grabbed my hand and pulled me along behind her.

"And don't worry, Tiffani. They get big, like the Hulk, but they go back to normal... after."

Great. I hadn't slept with a man in five years, and it looked like I was going to be getting back on the proverbial wagon in a jail cell. In space. With a giant alien in beast mode. Why did my nipples tighten at the idea?

4

Tiffani, Bundar Prison, Block 4, Cell 11

I PULLED the hood closer and lower over my eyes, careful not to reveal the cuffs that felt like thousand-pound weights on my wrists. They were nothing of the sort, but I couldn't forget about them, or what they meant. We were somewhere called Block 4. I had no idea how many sections of prisoners they kept here; most of the cells we'd passed in a different block had been empty.

But not these.

Naked giants lounged in the cells, and with each of them I walked by, my anger grew. I felt like I was walking by tigers caged at a zoo. The Atlan warriors were all huge, their shoulders just as broad as those of Warlord Dax as I followed him down the sterile, cream-colored corridors. Some were Dax's size, but others must have been in their beast mode. They were half a foot taller still, their muscles bulging to the point they didn't look like they could be real. Their bodies were magnificent, rippling muscle so well defined I could trace the outline of each individual tendon and connection with my eyes. They truly looked like gods among men, but their faces? Fierce, predatory eyes, long pointed teeth and their focus on me, as I passed by, so complete that when one growled and rushed the front of his cell, I jumped and lost my balance.

Warlord Dax was there, catching me before I fell and setting me back on my feet. All that separated me from the wild men was some kind of bright force field. It flashed bright blue as the beast man charged at me again. The power of it made him fly backward with a howl of pain where he crouched like an animal, watching me.

I was safe, protected by the invisible barrier. It was better than bars of a prison cell on Earth, stronger.

God, was this what I was about to deal with? Was an Atlan like *that* who I was supposed to give myself to as a mate? To trust not to hurt me? Oh, shit.

"Is that him?" I whispered.

Dax released me, and I almost wished he hadn't; the gentle heat of his huge hands helped prevent me panicking. "No."

Sarah shook her head and rushed to take my hand. I was relieved they were with me. How could I do this? How could I have even thought I could just fuck my mate out of his beast mode? Clearly I'd been delusional about what *beast mode* meant.

"Shhh," Sarah replied. "He's in eleven. Remember."

Yes, now I did. Dax began walking again and I fell in behind him, Sarah's arm linked with mine in a show of moral support that I desperately needed. Perhaps she was also holding on to me so I wouldn't change my mind and run away. My mate was their friend and they didn't want to see him executed. If I could save him, they would probably drag me kicking and screaming down the long corridor if need be.

"He won't be like that. He can't be. I promise," Sarah vowed.

A shudder raced through my body and I nibbled on my bottom lip. If that was what an Atlan male was like after they lost control of their beast, a wild... *thing* inside them, suddenly the whole execution thing made a lot more sense. "How do you know? When did you last see him?"

She squeezed my arm as Dax rounded a corner to the final cell. "Two days ago. He was talking then, and seemed mostly normal." She released her arm, gave me a quick hug and sighed. "Fingers crossed, Tiffani. Don't lose courage. Deek is not only a great commander, but a great warlord. A great Atlan. You'll get through this."

I didn't answer as I followed Dax and caught sight of my mate for the first time.

He was crouched in the center of the room, waiting for us, as if he'd heard us coming. He didn't growl or snarl, but his dark eyes inspected us with a predator's interest and I felt my hands begin to shake. Holy shit.

He was beautiful and even bigger than Dax, at least right now. Where the beast who'd just snarled at me moments ago scared the shit out of me, Deek's beast seemed calmer somehow, his body completely under his control. I could easily imagine him on a battlefield ripping his enemies in half with his bare hands. Throw a kilt and a broadsword across his back and every single woman on Earth would be panting with lust, despite the frightening display of teeth I saw when his eyes shifted to inspect me.

I knew he couldn't see much, not with the giant cloak practically swallowing me whole, but he didn't shift his gaze from me as Dax walked up to the force field. He glanced up at the corner nearest us to the imbedded surveillance camera I could just make out. It was small, no bigger than a dime-sized coin back home, but Sarah had told me it could see and hear everything that happened in that cell.

"Greetings, Commander."

"Dax." The beast moved then, uncurling from his crouch and stretching to his full height. He stepped forward, approaching, until the two warriors stood facing one another on opposite sides of the force field. A mixture of awe and nervousness had me take a step back. He towered over Dax by nearly a full head, standing close to eight feet tall. He was naked, too, his massive chest and thighs making me practically drool. His huge cock was on display, fully erect and ready.

Oh, God. That was ready for me. I was his mate and *that* was supposed to go in me! The thought caused my pussy to clench and the beast froze in place, sniffing the air as if he could smell my desire. Could he?

Dax drew a breath, as if to speak, but my mate cut him off and turned to look at me. I felt stripped naked and inspected, despite the heavy cloak.

"Who?" The word seemed to be a struggle for him, but he took a step sideways in his cell, shifting closer to me. The nearer he moved, the more my heart raced. I froze in place like a deer in headlights, my pussy soaking wet with those rough words. The sound of his voice made my nerves tingle and my breasts feel heavy. God, he was hot. Huge. Monster scary. So strong he could break me in half. And it turned me on. I wanted him more than anyone else before. It was instantaneous and heady.

And I was supposed to give myself to him, a complete stranger. Right now. And try to force the cuffs on his wrists when he wasn't looking. I felt like a six-week-old kitten contemplating taking on a fully grown tiger. No freaking way I was winning this one.

Sarah's hand came to rest on my shoulder and she leaned forward. I startled at the touch and took a deep breath, knowing I had to calm down in order to do this.

"Trust me. He's already interested. See how he's watching you. He's your match. He's yours, Tiffani. And you are his. His beast will know it, perhaps already does, even if he doesn't. You can do this."

I can do this. I can do this. I can do this. I chanted the words in my head, drowning out all other thoughts as I forced myself to calm down. I ignored his size and simply looked at his body, which was magnificent. His cock was long and thick—bigger than any I'd seen before—a dark plum color with a large, flared head. A thick vein bulged along the length. I imagined it straining to reach me, to fill me. I imagined that colossal body lifting me like a toy and shoving me up against the wall, fucking my brains out, making me come. This creature was mine. By Earth law, Atlan law, and whatever crazy advanced science they used at the matching center to make sure we would be compatible. He was mine, and I wasn't going to let them kill him because I was too scared to let him take me now.

I can do this.

Deek took another step and I lifted my head and shoulders to look up at him. His gaze had softened from those of a hunter about to kill to something far more interesting but no less intense.

Lifting my hands, I glanced to Warlord Dax for permission. He glanced at the surveillance camera, which was now blinking with a strange yellow light, and turned back to me with a nod. "Go ahead, Tiffani. The system is down."

"Tiffani." Deek's voice was rough and deep, reminding me of the garbled sound of a voice coming through a bass speaker.

I lowered my hood and turned my face up to my mate. "Hello, Deek."

He didn't answer with words, but a low, rumbling growl filled the space, the sound so loud it reverberated through my chest like a dance beat at a raging club. He stared and I could not break eye contact, no matter how much I wanted to look away. I felt hypnotized.

When we simply stared at one another, my heart about to pound itself right out of my ribcage, Dax stepped forward. "Do you want us to let her in, Commander? You've refused all the others."

In response to Dax's question, my mate backed away from the force field and my heart sank. Damn. He was big and scary as hell, but he didn't want me after all. Even raging with fever and execution looming, he refused.

When he was all the way at the back of the cell, next to a large bed, he turned and placed his hands flat above his head on the cell wall. I turned to Dax. "What is he doing?"

Dax's smile was genuine, and I relaxed. "He must face the back of his cell with his arms on the wall before I can lower the force field. It's protocol, to protect the guards and visitors." Dax's smile faded and he glanced from Deek's muscled frame back to me. "Be careful, Tiffani. He's not human. He won't want to hurt you, I know him, but be gentle with him."

"Gentle?" Was he fucking kidding me? Me? Be gentle?

Sarah jumped excitedly. "Quick, let her in!"

I glanced at Sarah, the question Dax had asked Deek a moment ago finally registering through the fog of lust and fear in my brain. "What others did he refuse?"

She rolled her eyes. "A ton of women have been in here, throwing themselves at him. When they go beast mode, Atlan woman willing to take them as a mate are paraded through here like models on a runway. If any of the men react, the women are put in the cell to try to claim them as mates."

I turned back to watch Deek, his hands flexing into fists against the wall over and over, as if he was fighting for control. "Does it work?"

"Sometimes. But not for the commander. He's refused at least twenty females, including his betrothed."

"His what?" Had I heard that right? His betrothed? Anger and jealousy stirred as I inspected my mate. He was mine, not some betrothed. All that beastly hotness was fucking mine.

Sarah waved her hands in an apologetic gesture. "It doesn't matter."

"Doesn't matter?" I asked, my eyes wide. "He has a betrothed and it doesn't matter?"

Sarah swiped her hand through the air. "A mate trumps a betrothed, Tiffani. If an Atlan doesn't find his true mate, he can marry someone else and hope the beast will accept them, which they usually do, as long as he's not in mating fever. Tia is his 'fallback' woman. At least that's how I think of it. But Deek won't need a fallback because you're his mate. He's yours."

"The force field will be down for three seconds, Tiffani. When I give the command, you must enter his cell completely and without delay," Dax instructed.

Warlord Dax moved to the far side of the cell's wall and placed his palm on a small scanner in the corridor.

I nodded, numb. This was about to happen. I was about to be locked inside that cell with a beast who could barely speak. It was the stupid betrothed female, the jealousy of her, that had me ready to claim my mate. No one would take Deek from me. No stupid Atlan woman was going to fuck this up for me. No *betrothed.*

A strange humming sound filled the air, then a silence made profound by its absence.

"Now!" Warlord Dax barked the order at me and my body jolted forward of its own accord, my legs moving me over the thin demarcation in the floor and into Deek's cell. The buzzing resumed and I turned to look over my shoulder at Sarah, whose dark eyes were filled with hope and sympathy. "Good luck, Tiff. The security camera will be down until the guards change shift."

"When is that?" I asked. I knew I was going to have to have sex with a complete stranger who was nowhere close to human, but I sure as hell didn't need an audience.

Warlord Dax wrapped his arm around Sarah's waist. "You've got five hours, Tiffani Wilson of Earth. Please, help him if you can."

What he meant to say was, *Fuck the warrior until you can't walk right for a week, but be sure to soothe his beast. Oh, and if the commander loses control, he might accidentally kill you. Sorry about that.*

I licked my dry lips. "I will."

My only two allies on this strange new world turned and walked away. My heart moved upward and into my throat, making it difficult to swallow. I watched until they were gone, my eyes burning with unshed tears as adrenaline, fear, anticipation, desire, hope and dread all coalesced into a tornado of emotion behind my eyes.

And then I heard him. My mate behind me.

Tensing, I turned to see him moving toward me like a hunter, slowly, carefully, controlled so I wouldn't bolt. With a sigh, I decided either I could be scared to death, or I could trust what Warden Egara told me. If he was mine, he would know. He would listen to me. He wouldn't hurt me. He wouldn't wrap those gigantic hands around my neck and snap me like a twig. Nope.

I reached into the pockets of my cloak and pulled his matching cuffs from within. Assured by the heavy gold bands in my palm, I undid the clasp at my throat and let the heavy garment drop to my feet.

Deek stilled, frozen in place as I stepped away from the fallen cover; my Atlan dress wrapped my breasts in a tight golden crisscross, which put the large orbs on perfect display. The V-neck style showed a lot of skin, and his breathing hitched as he inspected me, his hungry gaze raking over every inch of my body, from my slippered feet to the top of my head. But when his gaze reached the cuffs on my wrists and the matching ones in my palm, he roared, rushing me.

Before I could blink, I was backed against the wall, his large body pressing me close and holding me in place. "Cuffs. Mate."

A rush of exhilaration shot through me when he recognized the cuffs, understood the significance of them. When he leaned down and ran his tongue along my neck, my collarbone, between my cleavage, like he was feasting on my body, I sighed, relieved and very, very aroused. Up close, he was even bigger than I'd imagined. I wasn't a short woman and was never considered *small*. I felt dwarfed by him, feminine. Even his cock was big. God, his hard cock was like an iron branding the skin of my stomach.

He lifted my hands above my head and secured both of my wrists in a strong grip, his much larger cuffs dangling from my grip, but I would not let go. I needed him to wear the cuffs, to put them on his wrists.

The metal cuffs struck one another, the ringing sound of metal striking metal distinct in the warm air. With my arms above my head and his massive body before me, I was trapped, completely at his mercy. God, I really, really hoped I hadn't just made the biggest mistake of my life.

"Mate." He took his cuffs from my hand, held my arms trapped with one hand and lifted the cuffs up between us with the other.

I nodded my head against the hard wall, offered a breathy, "Yes."

Arms stretched above my head, I was on display, my ample breasts thrusting forward, cushioning his enormous chest. I couldn't answer, not without my voice cracking with pain. He was so damn beautiful, so big and fierce and perfectly formed. The moment I'd seen him, I wanted him.

He lifted his head, his harsh breathing the only sound in the sterile space. I opened my eyes, tilted my chin up, to find the beast watching me intently.

"Need," he growled. "Fuck you."

Shocked, I realized he was asking for permission. This

beast of a man was actually asking for permission. Even in his fevered, wild state, he was making me consent. My hands were restrained, but I knew he'd release me, let me go if I had changed my mind. And that made me even hotter and wetter for him. I'd been hot for him since that crazy dream in the bride processing center. I licked my lips, my breath hitching. But he didn't want to mate me, only fuck. Well, if nothing else, I was about to get the ride of a lifetime.

His cock was hard and hot, pressed between us and suddenly I wanted nothing more than to wrap my legs around his waist and take him for a ride. He was my mate and I wasn't going to deny that, no matter how much he did. I could fuck him now, hopefully soothe the beast, then make him see reason when his mind was clear.

"Yes," I breathed. "I want you inside me."

I did. I needed this so badly.

He growled and turned me to face the wall, just like I'd been in my dream. He released his hold on my wrists but when I tried to move, I could not pull my arms free, the golden cuffs now locked somehow to a metal device in the wall I'd not noticed before. Tugging, there was no give. I was the prisoner now.

Even with his cuffs in his hands, he easily stripped the dress from my body, letting it pool at my feet. The cool air of the room only made the heat emanating from him only that much hotter. I felt it against my back.

I waited, expecting him to position his cock at my core and thrust deep. Instead, Deek's hands roamed my body, cupping and teasing my heavy breasts, massaging my thighs and ass. His firm touch explored every inch of me, from the top of my smallest toe to the curve of my stomach, the arch of my brow, and all the while a low rumble built in his chest, the sound exciting me until wet welcome coated my thighs. My pussy was so hot it throbbed with each beat of my heart, the thumping need making me desperate to be filled, desperate for release.

"Do it already," I commanded, out of patience. I'd transported across the galaxy to save this man, and now he wanted to play touchy-feely when I was so empty I wanted to sob. I'd never been like this before, never needed or wanted so desperately. "God, please. Just fuck me."

Smack!

Smack!

Smack!

Fire raced through my bloodstream as his firm hand landed on my bare ass, the crack of the fast, fiery spanking making me shudder, first with shock, then with need. "Deek!" I cried. "What are you doing?"

I looked over my shoulder and watched as his palm lifted and spanked again and again.

Smack!

Smack!

Smack!

"No orders." He struck the opposite side of my bare bottom and I wilted like an orchid on hot asphalt.

No orders. From what Dax said, he was a commander, a leader of his own battalion of warriors. He liked to be in charge, and it seemed that pertained to me, too. I melted under his command, something inside me erupting to wrestle control of my body away from my mind, to submit. I was trapped, completely at his mercy, and the knowledge made my body surrender to his will utterly and completely.

With a whimper, my legs collapsed and I hung from the bands around my wrists. Instantly, he lifted me, taking my weight. With a strength I'd never dared imagine in a man, he turned me in his arms to face him.

"Mine."

He stared down into my eyes as he lifted me. I was naked and he shifted, the broad head of his cock nestling at my entrance. Without delay, he filled me, slowly, opening me wide, then thrusting deep.

ommander Deek

MY HEAD CLEARED as my cock sank into her soft body, as if a swirling fog had been lifted. Was her slick arousal the antidote to the fever as everyone said? Was it just the hot, tight feel of her that eased my beast, tempered its need? I would discover the reasoning later. Now, now she was perfect in my arms, her softness like a balm to my beast's rage. And she was soft everywhere, from her large breasts to the fullness of her ass and thighs. So soft, I felt as if I melted into her, was welcomed by her in a way no other had ever accepted me before.

I stared down into her passion-filled green eyes and knew she was not from my world. She was human, like Dax's little mate.

Mate.

The beast liked that word, liked the scent of her, the feel

of her skin, the taste of her, the tight feel of her pussy. I wanted to savor every inch of her perfect body, but the beast would not relinquish control.

He was angry at being pent up and imprisoned, refusing to give in until he'd fucked her and filled her with his seed.

Tiffani.

I didn't know how she'd gotten here, or what insanity had inspired her to come inside my containment cell.

The beast didn't care. He wanted to fuck. And based on the glazed look in the female's eyes, so did she. Gods, so did I. She was mine. The cuffs on her wrists proved it. I would recognize my family's pattern in the metal anywhere. I would question how she came to wear them later. So many questions.

For now, she wore my cuffs and that meant she'd chosen to do so. She'd chosen to be mine. Chosen my seed to fill her and bond her to me.

Mine.

I gripped the metal cuffs that had heated in my firm grip, their presence offering me a sense of hope, of calm. While the beast wanted to fill her with seed and mark her, I needed to make her mine as well. Let her see that I was choosing her just as readily. While my cock was nestled deep inside her, indicating that my beast wanted her, I opened one cuff and I wrapped it about my wrist, the seal closing automatically. I felt it tighten and become snug as I put on the other.

Awareness flowed through me. It wasn't a mental bond like the Prillons had with their mates. It was elemental. The knowledge that this Earth female and I wore the same cuffs, that we could not be separated without pain, without fucking and mating, was heady. Crucial. Life or death.

I knew it, somehow. Deep down. I didn't need my beast to prowl and pace, to nudge me into her, to nuzzle her neck and scent her. To lick her skin and taste her. To fuck and fill her.

She was mine, and my beast's. Her eyes flared with awareness, of acceptance and she clenched down on my cock, her pussy almost weeping with her copious arousal.

I dragged my gaze from her pink lips, her lovely face, lower, where her full breasts were bare to my hungry gaze. She was shorter than an Atlan woman, but lush, her large breasts spilling over my hands as I cupped them and played with her pink nipples. Her body was full, round and so soft, so extraordinarily soft everywhere, her skin more supple than the most delicate flower petals in my sister's garden.

Lowering my head, careful of the beast's teeth, I claimed her mouth as I filled her pussy. Kissing her was incredible. Her tongue mated with mine, her flavor hot and spicy. It only made me want to taste her everywhere, to drop to my knees and lick up wet heat, taste her on my tongue.

And so I did. She whimpered when my cock slipped free and I dropped to my knees before her. My beast growled, missing the tight heat of her pussy. But the beast was no longer in control. I was. I was able to push back the wildness, the raging fever, to think and command my strength once more. I was still in beast mode, my body transformed into the giant warrior I needed to be to claim her properly.

"Mine." The word was barely more than a growl as I placed my hands on her thighs and nudged her legs apart. I kept them there on her taut muscles as I breathed in her woman's scent. I leaned in and ran my tongue along her slit, her whimper driving my mating fever to a new high.

But this time, the fire raging in my blood had an outlet.

My mate was here. I was in control of my beast. This time, I would command my mate's body to come over and over.

My beast growled as her flavor burst on my tongue. It was no longer angry, only eager for more. And so I worked her with my tongue, my lips, sucking and licking, laving her clit with attention, learning how she liked it, what made her hips shift, caused her breath to escape in mewling little pants.

I slipped a finger into her honeyed depths, finding that spongy little spot that set her off, had her screaming her pleasure as she writhed and rode my finger. My hand on her thigh held her still as I licked and flicked at her clit until she came down from her pleasure.

Only then did I kiss my way up her body, suckling one nipple and then the other, until I took her mouth once again. This time, she was soft and pliant, her kiss more languid desire than desperate need. I'd made her this way. I'd given her the orgasm she needed. And I'd do it again.

Grabbing the back of her thighs, I lifted her so she wrapped her legs about my waist. My cock slid right through her folds into her. Nothing was stopping me now. My beast and I were in sync. It was time to fuck, time to take, but the way she was crying out *yes, yes, yes* with each thrust, she wasn't just giving. She was taking her own pleasure from my cock.

Her pussy clenched down on my cock like a fist as she came again, milking me, pulling me in deeper.

She was mindless now, her hands fisted above the restraints. Her eyes were closed, her cheeks flushed. Her breasts bounced and swayed as I filled her. I could feel my orgasm building at the base of my spine, my balls tightening, my seed ready to burst forth.

Leaning down, I kissed her neck, licked her salty, sweaty skin. Breathed her in as she continued to come.

It was the rippling of her pussy that finished me off, that pushed the beast to thrust deep one last time and come. Pulse after pulse, I filled her with my seed. I growled out my pleasure, my eyes closed, my neck corded, every muscle in my body tense. My mind was lost to the exquisite pleasure that filled me, that I pumped into my mate.

She was mine. Fucked and marked. Cuffed. Claimed.

For the first time in days, I was eased. Soothed. The fever was gone and I was all Atlan with a contented beast well in hand. The wildness in my blood no longer paced and snarled, pushed and raged. It was content and sated, content that this woman's scent, her arousal, coated and surrounded it. Content to hold our mate in our arms and sink into her soft body, buried in her gentle arms. For even as I thrust one last time, just to feel the firm pressure of her pussy squeezing my cock, she stroked me with her legs, her delicate little feet running up and down the back of my ass and thighs, as if she needed to touch me, to explore me as well.

Reaching up, I released the restraints about her wrists, let her arms drop as I continued to hold her against the wall, safe and secure in my arms. Her hands lifted immediately to my head and she buried her fingers in my hair, stroking me, petting me, letting me know she was all right and claiming me as her own. The knowledge that my cuffs were firmly about her wrists, that no one could take her from me, settled my beast as nothing else could have.

For the first time in a week, I was Commander Deek again. While I'd had thousands of warriors under my command in the Coalition Fleet, their obedience meant nothing when compared to this one woman's willing submission. I had fought, and would have died for those warriors.

But for this woman, this stranger, my beautiful mate, I would do anything.

The cuffs around my wrist declared it to all of Atlan.

Man and beast, she owned me now.

TIFFANI

OH, my God. I'd never... I mean, I'd come before, but never like that. Holy shit. I tried to catch my breath, to let my mind catch up to what he'd done to my body. My body.

I clenched down on Deek's cock, felt his seed slip around it and down my thighs. The feel of his hips pounding into mine, the grip of his hands against my bottom where he'd spanked me—

He'd spanked me!

And I'd loved it. All of it. He truly was an Atlan warrior, for he'd commanded me, with only a few words, to give over to his authority, to his control of my body. He wasn't mind-less about it. In fact, he'd been quite intent. When his cock filled me for the first time, I saw a shift in his eyes. They went from dark pools of animalistic need, completely blind to reality, to awareness. It was as if my body had relieved him of whatever ailed him.

I'd been told, time and again, that I was the only one to soothe his beast. Sarah had insisted I would have to seduce him, fuck him back to himself. But I doubted. Deep in my heart I'd still believed the true soothing would come from gentle words or perhaps a hand tenderly stroking his cheek, the running of my fingertips through his dark hair. But I hadn't really understood. Dax had tried to warn me.

"He's not human."

No. My mate was not human. And his taming had come from a different kind of stroke, that of his cock deep inside my pussy. My surrender had been the medicine he'd needed.

God, did my pussy have special powers? Super-Pussy! I needed a cape or something to go along with my new super-hero name. I couldn't help but grin against his broad chest at the absurd idea.

Deek carefully lowered my legs and slipped from me. I couldn't help but hiss at the slight ache. My body was not accustomed to being fucked—it had been a long time. I'd also never taken such a big cock, had one so skillfully used before. I wasn't complaining. The twinge of discomfort only made me feel more feminine, more powerful.

Without another word, Deek lifted me in his arms as if I weighed nothing, and carried me to his large bed. There, he laid me down and wrapped his arms around me, the giant beast at my back making me feel safe and secure. Nothing would reach me while I was with him. Nothing would hurt me. He was mine.

And I was his now.

He nuzzled my neck and pulled my back to his chest, his body wrapped around me, his back to the force field and the camera at the front of the cell. As his heat sank into my body I realized just how exhausted I was. Between the flight to the bride processing center, my arrival at Dax and Sarah's castle, and anxiety over how this meeting with my mate would go, I was so tired I could barely keep my eyes open.

"Sleep."

And just as my body obeyed when he touched me, my eyes drifted closed and I slipped away to dream.

TIFFANI

I WOKE SLOWLY, so warm, so comfortable, that I didn't want to move. A hard cock pressed to my ass, sliding over my pussy lips in a slow, heated glide. When Deek lifted my leg up, behind me, over his hip, I did not resist. Nor did I resist the hard thrust of his cock filling me from behind. His huge cock spread me open, his hand like an iron band around my thigh, holding me open for him.

The hand on my thigh slipped lower, kneading the soft roundness of my abdomen with a low rumble that made my pussy slick with a fresh rush of need.

I heard a rumble from Deek's chest just before a blunt finger slid lower, through the wet folds of my pussy to rub my clit as he fucked me slowly, thrusting in and out of my body as if he had hours to tease me, fuck me, make me beg.

I could smell our combined essence, the mixture of my body's wetness and his seed where it smeared on the insides of my thighs. He rubbed the wetness into my skin, as if marking me with his scent. Once he appeared to be satisfied, he shifted his attention to my breasts, cupping one full lobe with his huge hand, running his thumb over the hardening peak of my nipple. I gasped as his cock thickened inside me at the carnal touch.

"Who are you, Tiffani?" Deek asked, his voice deep and rough in my ear, but a man's voice.

Turning to look over my shoulder, I glanced up at him—way up, for he was so much taller—and saw that he was smaller, his shoulders not quite as broad, his face, his terrifying teeth now looked almost... normal. Big, larger than any man I'd ever known, but no longer quite so frightening. His eyes, a deep forest green rimmed with gold, seemed to be enthralled by his actions, by watching my body's heated response to his touch.

"My name is Tiffani Wilson. I'm twenty-seven. I'm from Earth." Uncertain of what he expected me to say, I started rambling. "My dad was a cop."

"What is cop?"

"Um, the police. Law enforcement?"

Deek nodded and pumped slowly, so slowly, in and out of me, as if fucking and talking were completely normal. "He was a warrior. A protector? That is why you are so brave."

"I'm not brave, Deek. But, yes, I guess I learned a lot from him. I respect the law. My mom—"

He shifted his hips and rolled my nipple in his fingers. With a gasp, I tried to finish my sentence. "My mom worked odd jobs, but mostly stayed home to take care of me when I was little. At least until he died."

In. Out. He lifted my leg a bit higher, thrust three times hard and fast. When I closed my eyes, he stopped moving.

"Tiffani."

"Hmm?"

"Tell me more. I want to know you."

"I can't think when you..."

"Do this?" He started fucking me again, moving slowly.

"Yes."

He chuckled in my ear and nibbled on my jaw. "Good. But keep talking anyway. Consider it a personal challenge."

I smiled, and my heart melted a little for this stranger. At least he appeared to have a sense of humor. I'd never had anyone play in bed before. The few lovers I'd had had been much more interested in getting in, getting off, and getting out. This was a new experience for me. And it was... fun.

God, I'd never once thought sex could actually be fun.

His deep voice rumbled through me as he cupped my breast, kneading the soft mass in his huge hand. "Do you accept my challenge, or should I stop?"

"Stop what?"

"Fucking you."

Oh, hell no. "Don't stop."

"Then, please, tell me more."

"My dad had a heart attack when I was fourteen. My mom started drinking and I barely finished high school before she kicked me out."

"That is not honorable."

I sighed. "She was broken. It was a rough few years, but we got over it. She's gone now, too."

"You were alone on your Earth?"

"Yes." Alone didn't even begin to describe the long, lonely nights after a hard day's work. The back-stabbing, skinny bitches at the diner talking shit about me even though I worked circles around them. Watching my friends from high school go off to college, get married and start having kids. The mean comments I got for being big when I went shopping, or walked down the street. Alone? Isolated? Lonely? Yeah. You could say that.

His touch gentled and he stroked my stomach, petting

me as if trying to take my pain. I had to admit, it was totally working and I melted into his body, completely relaxed, languid as he took me, filled me, made me feel like I was important, beautiful. Loved.

A tear slid, hot and wet, down my cheek into the sheets and I ignored it, biting my lip to stop the coming flood. I had no idea feeling loved would hurt this much.

He prompted me out of my silence. "What did you like to do on Earth?"

"I was a waitress." I had no idea if he would know what that meant, so I clarified. "I served people food."

"A caregiver. I am not surprised. Did you enjoy this work?"

I choked on my laughter. "No. Not really."

"Then you will not do that work here."

Just like that, as if he could solve all of my life problems with his will alone. At the moment, I didn't care about any of that. My body was spiraling higher and higher. My core was so sensitive, so swollen, that each stroke of his cock was like a jolt of electricity through my body. I needed him to focus here. Enough talking. I tightened my inner muscles and felt a small shudder pass through the massive muscles of his chest where they pressed to my back. So, I did it again.

"I'm... I'm your matched mate, Deek. You're mine."

"Mine." His deep growl sounded much more like beast than man.

Yes! His fingers moved to my other nipple and I watched as he lowered his head, gently licking my shoulder, burying his nose in my hair, breathing me in as his hand slid back down to my clit, teasing me with a gentle exploration that I had no hope of resisting.

He stroked my clit, plucked my nipples, rubbed my body

without hesitation, learning every inch of me, branding me as his, all as his cock thrust deep, in and out, fast, then slow. And every moment he watched me as if fascinated.

My orgasm rolled through me out of nowhere, my body languid and relaxed in his hands one moment, lost to the fire of my orgasm the next. And still he watched, his fingers relentless now, forcing another orgasm from my sated body as he thrust hard and deep, his pace lost to frantic thrusting that pushed me over the edge as he came deep inside me, his seed coating my pussy with his claim.

He held me still, trapped in front of him as our breathing returned to normal. I lay with his cock still inside me, his massive frame making me feel protected and feminine, wanted.

And still, a question burned through the sensual haze fogging my brain. A very important question. "Are we mated now? Are you... is your beast... are you all right?"

The harsh light from the cell reflected off the metal locked around his wrist and I lifted my hand to grip his cuff. He lifted his head from my shoulder and our eyes met. "Yes, we are mated now. My seed filled you while I was in beast form. The family cuffs are on our wrists. There is no question as to that. But how did you get here?"

"I can answer that."

Deek moved quickly, too quickly for me to comprehend, sliding his cock from my body and shielding my nakedness from the man who'd answered Deek's question.

"Dax," Deek said.

I sucked in a breath, realizing that the other Atlan warrior stood just outside the force field and could see me. *Had.* He *had* been able to see me, but no longer. Deek's body shielded me entirely.

"Turn away, Dax. I would cover my mate."

"Of course."

I couldn't see what was happening, but Dax must have turned his back. Deek reached over onto the floor and picked up my discarded cloak. When he had the garment open and ready, he wrapped it around me.

He looked down at me, his eyes once again honed to a warrior's sharp attention. "No one will see you. Your body belongs to me."

His words only made me hot. I shouldn't want to feel possessed by someone else, have someone stake a claim on me, for it went against every feminine principle I'd held dear. But from Deek's lips, they were protective and... God, perfect. I *wanted* to be possessed by him, for there was no question he was possessed by me. A mating was different than picking up some hot guy at a bar back home. I could sense our connection, could feel it in my pussy and down my thighs.

He spun back around once I gripped the cloak about me, covering me once again from head to toe, only this time I was naked beneath, my dress still a small pile on the floor.

"Warlord, explain yourself," Deek commanded, his shoulders back, his bearing that of a true leader. Even naked, he was magnificent and demanding. While I held tightly to my modesty, it seemed Deek had none.

"While on the *Battleship Brekk*, before your transport here, I put you through the Coalition Bride protocols for testing. Just as you did for me. If you were to be executed, I knew there was only one woman in the universe who could release you from your mating fever."

Deek pulled me forward so I was by his side, his arm wrapped securely about my waist.

Dax and Sarah stood on the other side of the force field, appearing just as they had when they'd left. How long ago had it been? They seemed more relaxed now, less tense, but their eyes held questions.

"Tiffani," Deek replied. "My matched mate." I liked the way my name sounded in his deep voice.

Dax nodded. "She is one feisty female. She forced the Bride Program to transport her, adamant that she could—and would—save you."

He looked down at me with a hint of awe and respect in his sated gaze.

"Which she has."

When Dax exhaled loudly, I turned to look at him. Sarah took his hand and she smiled. He did, too. I realized then that they hadn't known the mating had succeeded in soothing the beast, in ending the mating fever. They only knew that I was their friend's last chance for survival.

"I see the cuffs on your wrists."

Deek held one up at Dax's statement, stared at it, then grinned. "My beast is soothed. I am—" he glanced down at me with a look of reverence, "—claimed."

"Guards!" Dax shouted, his voice booming and echoing off the walls. "Guards," he repeated once again until he heard their heavy footfalls approach.

"Do not fear," Deek murmured in my ear. "You were so very brave. It is now my turn to take care of you."

I had never heard a man utter such words to me before. The comfort and shelter that they provided was like a balm. I hadn't realized how alone I'd been, how much I'd had to bear and handle without the support of... anyone. A lump formed in my throat as I blinked back tears.

The guards came then, turning Deek's attention away from me.

"Commander Deek's mating fever has been relieved. Release him at once," Dax ordered.

There were four guards similarly dressed in form-fitting armor like none I'd ever seen before. The strange material looked impenetrable, but it molded every muscle and plane of their bodies with amazing detail. The black and brown swirls, some type of camouflage I assumed, made them look immense and indestructible. I tried to imagine Deek's massive frame in such armor and very nearly groaned with desire. God, he'd look fucking hot.

Two guards approached, but the one with the most stripes on his chest and wrist stepped forward. He looked to Dax, who had issued the command, then to Deek. His eyes widened when he took me in on the wrong side of the force field wall.

"Commander," the man said.

Deek held up his free arm, showing him the cuff. "It is true. My mate is here and we have completed the mating bond. Summon the doctor to confirm my mating fever is gone."

The guard's gaze assessed Deek for a second, then flicked to me. I stared straight back at him, daring him to deny me. I wasn't leaving this cell without my mate.

He held my gaze for a few seconds before nodding. "Yes, Commander."

The doctor was quickly summoned and the force field was dropped to allow him access. Deek was quickly assessed by various objects with lights, but deemed well.

"You are quite lucky, Commander," the doctor said. He was not nearly the size of Deek, and his uniform was a dark shade of green that reminded me of pine trees and moss. The design was similar to the armored guards, but the material did not look hard, made for battle. It moved and flowed around his body with much more ease. His light brown hair had begun to turn gray at the temples and his dark gray eyes, as they assessed Deek, were completely focused and professional. I had no doubt this man had, at some point in time, been a warrior as well.

Deek returned to my side, wrapping his arm around my shoulders to pull me close. When he looked to me, he smiled. His formidable appearance shifted and I saw the gentle man beneath the commanding façade. "Yes, I am."

He kissed me then, in front of the doctor, the guards, Dax and Sarah, everyone, as if he was proud to be seen with me, eager for the world to know I belonged to him, and him alone.

Shock held me in place for long seconds before I responded. When I did, I let it all go, wrapping my arms around Deek's waist and pulling him close. His growl earned a chuckle from Dax, but Deek simply buried his huge hands in my hair and held me in place for a more thorough exploration.

The doctor cleared his throat. "I will sign the appropriate papers to repeal the order of execution. You are free to go."

Deek finally released me and I swayed, watching as the doctor looked over to where his guard stood at the edge of Deek's prison cell.

"Release him immediately."

My heart nearly leapt out of my chest with excitement and relief. I'd done it! Holy shit. I came to another world, seduced an alien and saved his life.

He was mine. All mine. The thought brought equal parts joy and anxiety. I had no idea who he was, what he thought, how he felt about anything. The warden at the bride processing center had promised he'd be perfect for me, and I really, really hoped she hadn't been lying.

What if he didn't like me? What if he thought my sense of humor was stupid. I loved wearing bright colors, lots of colors. What if he only wanted me to wear red, or black, or eat salad every day? What if he hated music? What if, now that he wasn't in mating fever, he decided he didn't want me?

I realized, truly realized for the first time, that I was about to go home with a complete stranger.

6

I FOLLOWED my little mate as she walked through her new house. I'd barely been in it, for I'd been stationed on *Battleship Brekk* for ten long years. Only on leave did I return. Until now, the large house had just been a place to sleep. But with my mate here, it suddenly felt like home.

Mine.

That one word seemed to be on a repeating loop in my mind. Every time I looked at Tiffani, caught a hint of her sweet scent, or remembered the tight heat of her pussy riding my cock, the word became a chant. *Mine.*

The beast might be soothed, I might now be able to control that part of me, but he lived within me still. Every time Tiffani drew near, he rose from the depths of my soul and fought to reach her, to touch her, to fuck her and mark her with his scent and his seed.

I'd heard other warriors speak of the beast's fierce devotion to their mates, but I'd never truly understood the overwhelming and primitive urge to protect, to fuck, to lie down at her feet and surrender my battered soul into her keeping.

I'd even shaken my head at the change in Dax since he'd been matched and mated to Sarah. Their connection was touching and the way the big warlord doted on his Earth mate was... endearing. And yet I'd assumed it would never happen to me. But here I was, mated to my own Earth female, and I realized I would do anything, *anything,* for her.

She'd already proven herself brave beyond belief. She'd refused the no-transport order and come across the galaxy. She'd risked breaking into my cell when she could have been arrested herself. She'd done it all to save me, a battered warrior she'd not yet met.

I'd never met anyone with so much compassion, such courage. I was quite sure I did not deserve her, yet knew I would kill to keep her by my side. She was mine, and I would never give her up.

Still, I was the commander. I was the one in charge. I did the saving.

But this woman had already humbled me in so many ways, and so had my beast.

The beast had seen many battles. I'd killed hundreds of Hive soldiers, ripped them limb from limb, watched them writhe and bleed and scream in agony. And the beast had felt nothing. Nothing but satisfaction as they died in pieces at my feet.

Now... now the cold-hearted monster within felt *everything.* For her. A woman I barely knew, an alien bride from a faraway world. A stranger.

"Do you like your new home, Tiffani?"

"It's beautiful." Her smile was shy as she ran her soft hand along the back of a large sofa in my bedroom suite and I realized it was one thing to fuck with mindless intent, to give the beast free rein over her body. But it was quite another to stand beside her, a man learning his mate, and try to set her at ease, to learn about her home, her past, about how she'd come to be mine.

The beast didn't care, his primeval heart not capable of such finesse. He saw. He wanted. He fucked. But that primitive nature would also protect her, for the beast would die to protect her, kill without a moment's hesitation to keep her safe.

As would I.

I walked to the window and the small table nestled just below. A bottle of our finest wine sat open and ready—a servant had prepared for our arrival—and I poured two glasses of the dark purple liquid, turning to offer one to my mate.

Our fingers grazed as she took it from me and the beast stirred with joy at that lightest of touches.

This woman had already wrecked me. I was hers, utterly and completely. I didn't need the cuffs about our wrists to convince me. Although she did not yet appear to understand the depths of their significance, or of my complete and unyielding devotion.

"Anything you want, mate, all you need do is ask."

"How about a superhero cape?" Her green eyes brightened with humor and I wished I knew her better, understood why she laughed.

I did not understand her reference, but would do what I could to please her. "I'll summon a tailor. I do not know to what you refer, but if you can draw it out, or explain it to him, he will make it for you."

She laughed, and the sound made something tight unravel in my chest. "That's all right. I wouldn't have anywhere to wear it." She sipped at her wine and looked up at me over the rim of her cup.

"Sarah has said she wishes to hold a party in celebration of our mating."

"You blush," I said, stating the obvious.

"I'm... embarrassed."

"For a party?" I asked.

She shook her head. "Because everyone will know what I did. What *we* did."

I frowned then. "No one will shame our union. They will think you brave and courageous, as I do."

She flushed even brighter, but she smiled.

"I'm not usually so brave," she admitted. "I usually just let things go, let people have their own way." She bit her lip and stared down into her wine; the sadness in her eyes made my heart ache. "Especially men."

"What are you talking about? Men on your world hurt you?" I asked, my eyes narrowing as the beast stirred, upset by her obvious hurt. The beast wanted to kill anything and anyone who'd dared hurt her. Ever. Which was stupid, irrational, and completely illogical, especially when those men were halfway across the galaxy on another planet.

She shook her head. "Not like you think. But I'm not a virgin. I tried—I wanted sex to mean something. But the men I chose, they had other ideas. I was never what they wanted." She looked up at me then, her deep green eyes haunted by the pain of rejection. Idiots.

My beast growled at the idea of her being used in such a

way. I grabbed her cuff, lifted her hand to my mouth, kissed the palm. "Never again. I want you, Tiffani. You are mine. Never doubt my desire for you."

She shook her head at the vehemence in my tone. "That's why I went to the Bride Processing Center. I wanted to find *the* one. To know that the match would be... perfect. She promised you would want me, that you wouldn't mind—"

"What? Finish your statement." The beast growled again.

"My size."

I lifted the wine from her hand and set both cups down on the table. Pulling her to me, I wrapped my arms around her, sank into her softness, and lowered my forehead to hers. "You are perfect. Do not worry that you are smaller than Atlan women. I love your body."

"I'm nowhere near small." Her cheeks blushed a deep shade of pink, but she held my gaze. "And you're the first to say that."

I lowered my head to her neck, tracing her jaw with my lips, enjoying a gentle exploration, the taste of her, the scent of her skin. "You are soft... everywhere." I placed a kiss atop her breasts, through her dress and lowered my hands to cup the nice, soft mounds of her ass. "I love how your body yields to mine, the way I sink into you, become one with you." I kissed her cheek, her forehead, her closed eyes. "I love your body. You are beautiful, Tiffani. Beautiful, and brave. You are everything I ever dreamed of in a mate and I look forward to spending the rest of my life learning everything about you."

She sighed and relaxed into my arms, as she meant to. Her surrender calmed my beast as nothing else had since we'd left the containment cell. But something bothered me about her words, something I found completely unacceptable in such a strong, beautiful woman.

A growl rumbled through me as the thought solidified. "You will have to forgive my inner beast, for it is quite protective and possessive of you. I find I share the same feelings."

"That's... nice to hear."

I kissed her, softly, quickly. "But you will never speak poorly of your body again. You will not doubt my desire, or your beauty. If you say such things again, I will take you over my knee and spank you, mate."

She shuddered in my arms, and I kissed her again, tasting her this time. I took my time, not to take her to bed, but simply to enjoy the way she felt in my arms. "Now, tell me about these men who hurt you."

"Oh, no. I wasn't really upset about bad boyfriends. It was just life, Deek. I was talking about bad bosses, bad jobs, bad landlords... I just had a lot of bad. I had to make a choice. Continue on with a dead-end job or do something about it. So here I am."

"Some of the Earth phrases don't translate with the NPU. I do not know what a dead-end job is or a landlord. Dax is a warlord but I doubt they are similar. Regardless, I understand what you were trying to say and I still find you incredibly brave." I kissed her on the tip of the nose. "And very, very beautiful."

She smiled then, exquisitely and brilliantly, and my beast calmed right down.

"What do you need now, mate? You saved my life. What can I do for you in return?"

She frowned then. "I didn't go to your cell and mate with you expecting some kind of payment or trade."

I'd offended her and my beast was petulant. I'd fucked up again and glanced down at the floor. I stood up to the Hive's worst fighters and I couldn't say the right thing with this Earth woman. "My apologies, Tiffani. I did not mean to offend. I just don't know what will please you. I am trying to learn."

"A bath might be nice," she replied. "You do have baths here on Atlan, don't you?"

My cock hardened instantly at the idea of her lush, round body sinking into a warm bath, of licking the moisture from her breasts, of running my soap-slicked hands over every ripe curve.

Lust must have clouded my gaze for her breathing changed in response to my desire, her gaze clouding with both heat and doubt.

"A bath. Yes. We have baths."

It seemed the beast knew exactly what to do to woo his mate, while I had no fucking clue what to do or say, stumbling over my words like an idiot youth. I had no finesse, no skill in basic conversation.

Grabbing my wine off the table, I drank the entire glass as I walked across the thick rug to the bathing chamber. I held open the door and turned to face her. "Here. You can... a bath..." I choked on what I would have said next as she walked toward me, her gaze soft and accepting.

"Great. Thank you." She winced slightly. "I'm a little... sticky."

I nodded, unable to speak. My cock hardened into a metal pole in my pants, knowing the stickiness she referred to was my seed. It was in her pussy, coating her, marking her. I felt virile and powerful and yet completely over-whelmed by her soft smile.

Fear. I was afraid, terrified that this woman would wake up, come to her senses and run. I was no gentle lover, no innocent young soldier. My body bore the scars of battle, as did my soul. And Tiffani? She was softness and light, the laughter and hope I desperately needed.

I doubted she needed me at all.

I could take good care of her, enjoying the spoils of war. While my beast mode had raged with incredible intensity, the mating fever had also been the cause of my immediate and permanent retirement from active duty in the Fleet. I was officially relieved of my command.

They'd expected me to be executed, but thankfully, I was now a mated warrior with the spoils that accompanied my high rank and years of service. The entire fifth wing of the family fortress was now mine, as well as two homes in the southern region. The Atlan council had granted me land and title, castles and wealth years ago when I came of age, hoping to lure me home before I was lost to the mating fever. The tactic had been successful on a few of my fellow warlords, those who had grown weary of battle and gone home to select a mate before their fevers struck.

But most, like me, did not want to leave their brothers on the battlefield. Only now, when forced, would I leave my command and settle into my new role on Atlan. Away from the front lines, I would now be granted a senior position on the war council to advise our warlords on ways to better prepare and train our new warriors before sending them into deep space to battle with the Coalition Fleet. The trainees would defend our world, and all worlds, against the deadly Hive menace.

But I'd served my time. Ten years was long enough. I was one of the few warriors lucky enough to survive, to return home to the comforts of a mate who, at this very moment, tugged her burgundy cloak closed around her lush body and turned away from me to enter the bathing chamber.

I followed her—as if I had a leash about my neck and she were tugging me along—and showed her how to operate the controls, to summon hot water and scented oils for her silken flesh. I noticed a new display of sexual toys along the wall, large and small, arranged to look like a tree with branches. Courtesy, no doubt, of my loyal staff, upon hearing I had taken a mate.

She barely glanced at them, and I forced my gaze back to the less tempting floor, marble tub, the dark ivory lighting recessed in the walls, anywhere but at her, or the toys I would use to bring her pleasure.

Turning abruptly, before I lost control, I left her, closing the door as softly as I could manage, the beast nearly growling at me to strip naked and join her in the giant tub, to take her again.

Wrestling the monster within me back under control, I could not resist listening to the sounds of her bath. I heard the soft rustle of clothing as her cloak hit the floor. Her soft sigh made my cock pulse as I imagined her lowering her naked body into the heated water.

Splashing sounds and her sweet, quiet voice hummed a haunting melody I assumed was from Earth, as I did not recognize the notes.

My knuckles were white where they curled around the arms of the chair outside the door. Yet I held myself in thrall, refused to push her. She'd saved my life already, her bravery something I had yet to completely fathom. She'd risked everything to transport across the galaxy to a mate she did not know, a mate in prison about to be executed. I owed her my life and my sanity, and I would never be able to repay her.

Proud of my control, I sat, staring at the door that separated me from what I most desired. Until she called for me.

"Deek? Are you there?"

I jumped up and stood, putting my hand on the door. The beast paced within and my voice turned deep, gravelly. "Yes. I would never leave you unprotected." The fierce vow was more beast than man, but in that, we were in complete agreement. My cuffs were a sign to everyone on Atlan, even on the battleships across the Coalition Fleet, that she was mine. No one dared touch the mate of an Atlan. Still, as my only prized possession, I would guard her fiercely.

The houses, the lavish properties hadn't meant a thing to me until she arrived. And now, they were still just things. Tiffani was everything.

I heard a trickle of water, a light splash. "I can practically feel you prowling around out there. Why don't you join me? I know you want to. Are you scared?"

While I could tell from her voice she was taunting me, I took it seriously. Was I scared? Yes. No. Fuck.

My mate was calling, inviting me to claim her, to bury my hard cock in her soft body, to lick the water from her skin.

The door was not locked and I swung it open slowly so I would not startle her. My mate had wet her hair, the gorgeous mass now nearly black and slicked back to reveal the gorgeous roundness of her face. Her lips looked fuller, her eyes larger as they watched me enter the small room. Where I was wary, she was completely at ease.

White marble surrounded her, the floor and tub a creamy white filled with swirls of gray and silver. The marble had come from the finest mines on Atlan. The bathing pool was large enough to fit both of us easily, and she swam to the back edge, farthest from me and placed her arms out to her sides, floating at the top of the water. Her cuffs winked at me, wet from the bath, and I could not stop the surge of satisfaction brought about by seeing my mark of ownership on her body. Her plump breasts floated in enchanting invitation, her pink nipples a darker red due to the heat of the water.

I pulled off the armored clothing Dax had given me at the prison, eager to wash the stench of the containment cell from my body. I'd endured until now because I also smelled like her.

My mate.

Her eyes tracked my every movement as I dropped my pants and stepped out of my boots. Completely naked now, I stood before her wearing nothing but the mating cuffs, nothing but the symbol of her claim over me, and allowed her to look her fill. My cock was erect, curving up toward my belly and her gaze finally focused there.

She was silent so long, I wasn't sure of my welcome, until she drew a shuddering breath. "God, you're hot."

"I am not hot, mate. The temperature in this room is adequate for our needs."

She chuckled. "Hot, as in sexy as hell. It's Earth slang for extremely fuckable."

So, my mate found me desirable. "You are the fuckable one, mate. My cock is hard as a rock every time I look at you." I took it in hand then, squeezed the base to stave off the need to lift her out of the water and take her right there, on the marble floor.

"All talk and no action." She rolled her eyes and beckoned me forward with one twitch of her finger. "If you want to fuck me, then get in here and do something about it."

My beast growled. Perhaps we weren't quite so different in our thinking as I'd believed.

"You liked it when I spanked you, didn't you?"

I thought of before, when my beast had taken over our mating and she'd been spanked for her bold actions, for taking such risks to save me. Perhaps I should have kissed her instead of spanking her, but I'd become instantly possessive and very protective of her. The beast also had wanted to be in control and it was not. It hadn't been since the first bout of fever came upon me. Because of this, it hadn't been gentle. He'd been demanding and expected submission. Now, with a clear head and a calm beast, I had to ensure I hadn't scared her, that she liked our encounter, that she wanted me just as rough and wild as my beast.

Her pupils dilated and she licked her lips. "Yes," she whispered.

"And when I restrained you?" I stepped down into the warm water. "Did your pussy get wet when I took control?"

A shudder racked her body. "Yes."

"I already knew the truth, but I needed to hear you say it aloud. We may be strangers, but we are matched mates. Eventually, we will know everything about each other. You will know what I like and I will know what you need." Tipping her chin up so her eyes met mine, I saw longing in her gaze, acceptance. Surrender.

"You want to be fucked, mate?"

"Yes," she said again, as if it were the only word she knew.

That one word broke my control and I sank into the water, pressed my hard cock to her stomach and claimed her mouth. Wrapping my arms around her, I lifted one arm behind her back to protect her from the sharp edge of the bathing pool and lowered my other to her wet pussy.

Two fingers. Deep. Hard. Fast.

She moaned into my mouth, the sound making my cock hurt. She was wet, so fucking wet I knew I had to taste her.

Lifting her in my arms, I turned and placed her so she sat on the edge of the pool, her back resting against the wall just a few inches behind her. Staring into her eyes, I slowly lifted one of her feet, placing it on the side of the tub, then the other until her pink pussy was on display, her glistening arousal a feast for my eyes.

The swirling bathwater had washed away my scent, my seed, and my beast rose up with a snarl, eager to mark her again. It did not like that we'd been washed away, that our scent did not cover her and could not protect her from amorous warriors who would take one look at her large, round breasts, her soft body, her lush thighs—and want to fuck her, take her, claim her. Again. And again.

"Why are you looking at me like that? You don't like—" Tiffani's voice was shaky and she lifted her legs, attempted to close them, to hide. "I'm sorry. I thought—I can't—never mind."

"No!" I snarled the word as I moved quickly to grab her knees with both hands and force her legs open wider. "No. Do not hide from me."

"But—"

I held her open and moved between her legs, my chest

pressing against her wet heat, her soft abdomen and thighs a cushion for my massive shoulders. "But what, Tiffani?"

"But I'm not... I mean, I'm sorry. Never mind. It's nothing." She turned her face away from me, her eyes dark... ashamed. The sight angered me.

"I warned you, mate."

"Warned me?"

Lifting her from the ledge, I pulled her into the water before laying her on her stomach. She lifted her hands to the edge of the bathing pool and held on, her ass perfectly on display where it floated above the water. "What did I say would happen if you doubted my desire, doubted your beauty?"

She shook her head. "I don't know."

Smack!

I spanked her plump, round ass and she squealed in surprise.

"That was for lying, mate. Now, tell me what I said would happen if you spoke of yourself in a negative way."

"That you'd spank me. You have to be kidding."

I rubbed her bottom, her back, telling her with my touch how gorgeous her body was, how perfect. "I will never make light of your perfection. Nor will I allow anyone to speak poorly of you." I tugged on her hair so she would turn her head and look at me. When our gazes locked, I spoke again. "Nor will I allow you to speak poorly of yourself."

Tears welled in her eyes and I released my hold, allowed her to turn away before I lost myself in her gaze, before I gave in and fucked her before giving her the solid reassurance she needed, comfort and security in the knowledge that I was in control, that I would honor her, defend her, protect her, even from herself.

Smack!

Smack!

Smack!

With each sharp strike of my palm on her naked flesh she writhed, her bottom turning a gorgeous shade of pink. I didn't spank her all that hard, but the sound of it in the tiled room was quite loud.

She turned her face to the side, her small teeth lightly sinking into the soft flesh of her arm.

Checking on her mental state, the response of her body, I lowered my touch to explore her wet folds and found her soft and slick, and not from water. But the spanking was not enough for my beast. He wanted complete dominance, ownership of her body in every way. He wanted complete submission. Tiffani needed to understand exactly who she belonged to now. Her body was mine. Her pleasure was mine. Her pussy, her breasts, her round bottom, soft skin and tight ass, mine. The beast rose and I knew my eyes were changing color, going black as night as my gaze roved over her pink bottom and full curves.

Mine. I agreed.

I reached above us to the wall, pulling down the smallest of the curved sex toys from its hook. Quickly coating both her tight rosette and the small end of the device with the scented oil, I spread open her pussy and slowly inserted the thick end of the curved device.

"Deek!" Her eyes went wide before closing in blissful surrender. "God, what are you doing?"

"Making sure you know who you belong to."

"I thought you were spanking me."

"I am, mate. I'm not finished with you yet."

Her only response was a soft moan as I slowly, so carefully worked my finger into her, coating her tight little hole. I moved the larger end of the device in and out of her wet heat, rotating the bulbous head over and over the ridge of resistance, the muscle within her core that I knew would bring her pleasure.

When I was sure she could take the rest, I removed my finger and slid the opposite end of the sexual device into her tight ass.

"Oh, God."

"Do you want me to stop?"

"No."

My beast snarled, and my next command was more growl than words. "Tell me if anything hurts."

She sobbed my name as I pulled back on the device and pushed back in, fucking her in both holes.

I kept it up until she was writhing, begging me to let her come.

And then I stopped with it deep inside her.

Smack!

Smack!

Smack!

"Who do you belong to?"

"You."

Smack!

Smack!

Smack!

"Say my name, Tiffani. I want to hear my name from your lips. I want you to know who is fucking you, who is pumping this hard rod into your ass, who is spanking you, worshipping you."

"Deek. Deek. Deek."

My name was a chant on her lips and I continued,

fucking her and spanking her until she went limp, shaking and desperate. Completely at my mercy. Mine to do with as I pleased. Her surrender complete.

The sight soothed both man and beast, and suddenly I couldn't wait to give her exactly what she wanted, to reward her for trusting me to take care of her, to give her what she needed.

"Do you want to come?"

"Please."

I pulled the toy from her body, freeing her for me. My mouth. My fingers. My hard cock.

I turned her over onto her back, lifted her and settled her once more on the edge of the tub. As before, I placed her feet to the sides, spreading her open for me. My gaze inspected every inch of skin, every freckle and curve, the lovely pink folds surrounding her core, the deep, dark chasm that waited, eager and empty, for my tongue or my cock. At the moment, I was having a very hard time deciding which to give her first.

She did not move, simply watched me and waited, submissive, defenseless, trusting.

My cock jerked beneath the water and my heart ached inside my chest. I'd never dreamed to see that expression, a surrender so complete, on the face of any woman.

My mate. Gods, she truly was perfect.

"Now, where were we?"

Her eyes were closed and she leaned her head back on the wall, accepting of whatever I would do to her body. She licked her lips, then spoke. "You were about to ravish me and make me forget everything and everyone but you."

I couldn't help my very possessive grin. "Exactly." I lowered my mouth to her pussy and thrust my tongue deep, claiming her in the most elemental way I could. Her gasps of pleasure, the wetness coating my tongue were all the encouragement I needed as I feasted on her feminine core. I used fingers and tongue, lips and teeth, tugging and sucking until I learned what made her gasp, hold her breath, shiver.

I slid two fingers into her pussy, fucking her as I sucked her clit, eager to push her to orgasm, to make her lose control. The tight center of her bottom beckoned, and I slowly worked a third finger inside her there, determined to claim her completely, everywhere.

"Mine," I whispered when she shifted to escape the new sensation.

"Deek!"

"Mine."

She settled and I resumed my assault on her clit, fucking her harder and faster with my hands as I increased the pressure and rhythm of my tongue. I worked her body until she screamed, the walls of her pussy fluttering in helpless spasms over my fingers.

Before it was over, I rose from the water onto the steps to align my cock with her eager pussy, then plunged deep, buried myself in the still pulsing heat of her.

I let the beast take over now that she'd found her pleasure, thrusting hard and deep, fucking her up against the wall like a wild thing as she tugged at me, pulling my hair, insisting I fuck her harder.

Faster.

Deeper.

I fucking loved her dirty talk, loved the way her cream coated my cock, the way her soft body jiggled with each solid lunge of my hips.

When she came again, her pussy tightening on me like a

fist, I finally let myself come, coating her with my scent, my seed.

The man in me insisted I would bathe her after, but the beast was in charge.

When he was done with her, he carried her to bed and held her, relished the idea of our child already taking root in her womb, our seed buried deep, our scent coating her lips, her pussy, her thighs.

∾

TIFFANI, one week later

"Do Atlans even have parties like this?" I asked Sarah.

It had been a week since Deek was cured of the mating fever. Days alone in his house and days of fucking. My body was sore in all the right places from his very ardent and eager attentions. It seemed he was as insatiable as I was.

The only reason he let me dress was because Sarah had banged on the front door, impatient to plan the event.

"It's not an engagement party, since you're already mated. It's not a wedding reception, since they don't have weddings," she replied. "But they do hold mating celebrations. I asked."

We were in Deek's kitchen—my kitchen, too, but I was not used to the idea—and Sarah was showing me how to cook using the odd machines. There was no fridge or blender or toaster. It was all different and I was thankful she understood my complete confusion. She'd come to Atlan from Earth only a short time ago.

Yes, we seemed to have servants constantly underfoot. But

if I got the munchies in the middle of the night, it would be really embarrassing to have to wake someone up to make me a snack. And I wasn't used to sitting around all day doing nothing. I'd worked fifty hours a week for years now and as much as I loved staying in bed with Deek, I was going to have to find something else to do. And party planning? Not really my thing.

"A mating reception? Everyone's just going to be celebrating that we... we slept together. That's it. It seems weird. It's too much." I picked up my mug of coffee to hide my embarrassment. Well, it was as close to coffee as they had on Atlan with dark beans from some plant I forgot the name of. Sarah had shown me how to make it, to add sweetener to it so it wasn't bitter. "And I don't know anyone here."

"You *are* mated, Tiff, and everyone knows how that happens." Sarah rolled her eyes and then laughed at me. "Seriously, it's no different than a wedding reception on Earth. How many brides are still virgins these days? The whole virginal white dress thing is a joke. With an Atlan, the fucking *is* the wedding. Now you get to have the party."

"Yes, but we aren't married. We just had sex. It seems weird to be having a party for it."

"A mating is more important than a wedding, Tiffani. There is no such thing as divorce here, or changing your mind. These guys mate for life."

I felt uncomfortable with the idea, just as I had days ago when Deek and I first talked about it. He didn't seem to be concerned, saying he was happy to show me off, to make the other warlords jealous. Of course, he didn't have a modest bone in his body. He was actually proud that I'd broken into his jail cell and fucked his brains out.

I, too, was proud of what I'd accomplished, but I wasn't

proud of what I'd had to do. I'd gone into a cell with a complete stranger and had sex with him.

To Deek, my actions were practically a badge of honor. I'd claimed him and then he'd restrained me and claimed me in return. Oh, and how he'd claimed me every day since! Knowing I liked to be tied up, he'd used the sash on my robe on more than one occasion to bind my hands together behind my back when he took me, or restrain me to the headboard of our bed.

Deek was inventive and very thorough. My nipples tightened just thinking about it.

"I know that look," Sarah said with a grin. She pulled a plate from a wall unit that had food on it, steam rising from the top. It smelled good, but it was nothing I'd ever seen before and I stared at the concoction she placed in front of me. Deek had served me food, obviously, but I hadn't paid much attention to it, for he'd been naked each and every time. But with Sarah serving—

"Goju root. You'll like it," she said, returning to the machine to get a plate of her own.

I pursed my lips and stared at the purple-colored vegetable. I only tasted it after she sat down and placed a forkful of her own inside her mouth.

My eyes widened at the sweet taste. "It tastes like... potatoes... with butter!"

Sarah pointed her fork at me. "Exactly!" She chewed and swallowed. "The party will be tomorrow night. Dax isn't keen on having it at our house, but only because he's never done it before. I assured him that he would be fine." She leaned in and whispered, as if her mate were nearby to overhear. "Atlan warlords aren't big partiers."

"Do I want to know how you assured him?" I waggled my eyebrows.

It was Sarah's turn to flush.

"You'll meet some Atlans and make friends. There will be other warriors' wives and of course, Tia. I think she's Deek's cousin twice removed or something."

I took another bite of the goju root. "Deek mentioned her and a few others who will be there. Her father, too. Angle or something."

"Engel Steen. Dax said he's a bigwig, in charge of all the supplies that go off world. He's rich, too. Fought in the Hive wars for a long time before he came home. Tia's his daughter. Apparently, Tia and Deek were promised to each other when they were kids, but then Deek never came back from the war in all those years, only being promoted and elected up the ranks. And when he finally did, he was in mating fever. Engel really wanted Tia to mate Deek, but Deek refused and Tia probably knew then that she wasn't his mate—if she wasn't aware of it before. Then you showed up."

"And ruined his master plan?" I put my fork down and took a drink of wine. Atlan didn't want for wine, which was great. It softened moments such as these when I wanted to take the fork in my hand and stick it in Tia's eye. I hadn't even met her, but I was insanely jealous of her having the slightest interest in Deek. Perhaps I had an inner beast of my own.

Sarah snorted. "I don't think trying to force an Atlan warlord, an elected field commander, no less, to do anything he doesn't want to do, is a master plan."

"What do you mean, elected? Don't they just get promoted, like normal soldiers?"

Sarah shook her head. "No way. The Atlans are hardcore badasses. If some puny human or Trion commander tried to give them orders on the battlefield, they'd probably get their heads ripped off. I saw Dax in action with the Hive. They're fucking scary when they fight."

"So, they elect their commanders?"

"Yep. And Deek was a commander over thousands of warriors. Which is why he's famous now, and super-rich."

Based on his house, it did seem that way, but Deek didn't seem to be one to flaunt it. Of course, I hadn't even left the house with him yet. Still, I'd struggled to get by after my parents died, spent my entire life living paycheck-to-paycheck. It was reassuring to know I didn't have to kill myself working at a deadbeat job for an asshole boss any longer.

"And every Atlan woman on the planet is going to hate my guts," I grumbled, poking at my Atlan potato substitute.

"Who cares? He wanted you." She took another bite, studying my sullen expression as she chewed her food, then swallowed. "They paraded a lot of women through that prison, Tiffani. He rejected every single one of them. Dax said Tia went down there multiple times. He just didn't want her. He wanted you."

"I still don't like her," I replied.

Sarah laughed. "I feel sorry for her. She's actually pretty nice... and harmless." Sarah's smile faded and I paid attention as she continued. "I don't think she really wanted him, either. She just didn't want him to die."

"That's... nice." It was, but a hollow fear seized me at how close Deek came to being executed and that made me like her more and want to like her even less all at the same time. "Yeah, well, I saved him and he's not going to die."

"Damn straight." Sarah picked up her wineglass and clinked it with mine.

"Let's figure out what you should wear tomorrow night and then I'll get going. I'm sure Deek is getting restless."

"And Dax?" I asked, a hint of laughter escaping as I thought of our two huge, intimidating mates huddled in the tiny office nearby, trying to give us some girl time, but unable to go far from our sides. They said it was because of the cuffs and the pain that would cause us if we were too far apart, but I think it was because they just wanted to be as close as possible.

"You know their beasts."

"I do?"

"Hell, yeah. They're insatiable. I know Dax can only allow me to hang with you for so long before he'll give in and track me down."

I grinned. "And then?"

She raised her glass once more. "And then, they make us come until we remember why we never want to leave their sides."

I clinked my glass to hers and we both sipped at our wine. Yes, my mate was quite possessive, not only of me but my time. I was thankful he understood my need to connect with Sarah, my only link to Earth. But she was right; Deek, like Dax, only had so much patience where I was concerned and he'd surely have me naked and begging again the moment we were alone.

My pussy clenched at the thought. God, yes, I loved being mated to an Atlan.

7

THE DREAM WAS INCREDIBLE. A female was on top of me, her light weight pressing me into the bed. Her skin was soft and smooth, the scent of her making my cock rise. She was kissing across my chest, her mouth a hot suction on one nipple, then lower, flicking into my navel. Lower still she moved until her nimble fingers opened my pants. Lifting my hips, I assisted with drawing them down, eager for her mouth on my cock. It was painfully erect, angry and dripping with my pre-cum.

She'd brought about my beast, and yet instead of pacing and snarling within, it was preening, agreeing with my Atlan mind that *this* was what we both wanted.

A good cock suck.

Her tongue circled the head, licking up my essence drop by drop. My fingers tangled in her hair, silky strands I held onto as I guided her onto my hard length and encouraged her to lower her head. To suck me deep. To take all of me in her hot, wet mouth.

The suction, gods, the suction and heat of her swirling tongue was too much. I arched my hips, pushing even deeper. It felt so good, my orgasm was building at the base of my spine. Cum boiled in my balls, tightening them, ready for release. I would spurt thick and hot over her tongue and down her throat.

Yes. Gods, *yes*.

My eyes flew open at the feel of the connection with this female. Lifting my head, I looked down my body to see her, my cock stretching her lush lips wide.

Tiffani. My beautiful, perfect mate. And she had my cock in her mouth.

With an audible pop, she released me. "Hello, mate."

Her voice was husky but soothing, the smile she offered was easy and just for me. I'd fallen asleep waiting for her. Sarah had come to our door, interrupting us—interrupting my time fucking my mate—but I saw Tiffani's eagerness to visit with someone from her home world. I could deny her nothing, even meeting with a new friend. And so I'd gone to my office and sat with Dax, hearing the two Earth women's laughter drift to me from the kitchen. I was happy that she was happy, but I'd taken her to bed the instant our friends left. She'd well and truly worn me out, bout after bout of lovemaking that was more draining than fighting the Hive. And so after I took her again, my seed deep inside her, I'd fallen asleep with a smile on my face and my beast sated, only to wake with my mate's mouth on my cock.

I was breathing hard, my need to come a pounding pressure in my balls. I looked at the cuffs about my wrists, incongruous to my fingers where they tangled in her hair. I saw the matching cuffs on her own wrists as her hands rested on my thighs. The cuffs marked her as mine. All mine. Her long brown hair pooled on top of my thigh as she took me back into her mouth. She fisted the base of my cock, moving hard and fast over the head, and I almost came right then. Release roared through me, but I held back. I wanted my cock in her pussy, my seed in her womb. I wanted my child growing inside her. I needed to know she was mine in every possible way.

"Tiffani. Stop."

She lifted her head and wrapped both hands around me, twisting them like a merciless little minx as I thrust into her tight grip.

"You fell asleep," she murmured. "And I wasn't done with you yet."

"Mmm," I replied. "I had a mate who wore me out, used my body and begged for orgasms until I was too tired to stay awake."

She smiled, had the look of a woman who knew her power over me. I might be the dominant one, but she had all the control. With her breath fanning my rock-hard cock, I'd do anything she wanted.

Relaxing her hold, she sat up. Holy fuck, she was naked and round, so fucking soft everywhere, so perfect. I groaned, unable to hold back my orgasm, my seed spurting hotly across my belly. Her eyes widened as she watched me come, pulse after thick pulse. I couldn't control it, couldn't deny the pleasure, for she'd pushed me to the brink with her hot mouth and then over the edge when she'd sat up and shown me her naked body. Lush, full breasts, tight nipples. Pale, creamy skin that was curved and perfect for my hands. I'd come like a randy youth.

She was too gorgeous. All I had to do was look at her, and I was lost.

"That's supposed to go inside me," she chided. She bit her lip and studied me as I caught my breath, the pleasure and relief from the orgasm slowing my brain to a sluggish halt.

And yet, she was staring at my cock, her hands still playing with the length, tracing its outline, its ridges, with her delicate fingers.

"Isn't it supposed to go down after you come?" she asked, staring at my still hard cock. It wasn't "going down" as she worded it, but instead hardening fully once again.

I grabbed the loose sheet and wiped my cum away. "Don't worry, I have plenty more. See what you do to me, mate?"

"Is your beast never soothed?" she asked.

I took a moment to consider my beast. It was tamed a bit, but it always was after an orgasm. But in the past few days, as Tiffani and I took time to learn each other—talking and fucking—the beast always wanted her. I never softened after just one orgasm, never seemed to break through the heated need that simmered just below the surface.

I thought of the other warlords I'd spoken to over the years, the Prillon warriors I saw on the battleships who took a mate. They'd all claim the desire for their mate was not like a fire, was not something that could ever be put out. No, the lust and need was more like a slowly boiling star. It would flare, shoot through the darkness of our battered souls like a storm, then ebb to the continual burn simply waiting to erupt again.

Tiffani was my world now, and I wanted her to understand that. I needed her to know the depth of my devotion to her already. I slowly shook my head and raised my hand gently to stroke the curve of her cheek.

When she pressed her face to my palm, I felt satisfaction that rivaled the feeling I had when she screamed my name, her pussy convulsing her pleasure on my cock. "Never, Tiffani. Neither beast nor man. Neither of us will ever get enough of you."

She blushed, the pretty pink color staining her cheeks. That I had expected. But I had also expected her to look away, to break the intensity of my gaze as I tried to absorb her essence with my eyes.

She did neither. Her dark green gaze held mine and the emotion I saw there caught my breath, surged to my cock like a lightning strike and made me instantly hard as iron in her hands.

"It is my job to soothe you," she said, her hand tightening around the base of my cock, stroking it with expert skill. "Let me do my job."

I growled at her bold behavior. Yes. I would lie here and let her have her way. I was unaccustomed to allowing someone to have control over me, but for Tiffani, I would submit. For now. Her sexual aggression, her desire for me was no less arousing. Yes, if she wanted to take charge, I'd give my body into her care. And so would my beast.

She worked me with hands and mouth, bringing me to the brink of orgasm just to release me before I could come deep in her throat. She'd tease me with her hands then, her lush lips exploring my body with nibbles and licks meant to push my limits. I realized, as she worked me to a fever pitch and held back time and again that she was testing me, testing my control.

She was trusting me not to lose it.

But my beast would not be denied. I couldn't hold back, couldn't resist her. She stroked me for a time, my hips bucking up for more. Her grip remained as she lifted a knee and straddled my hips, which opened her up so my cock nestled against her pussy.

"Your job?" I said, biting my lip to keep from coming. Again. "Fucking my mate is not a job." I sat up and began kissing along her shoulder. She whimpered.

"Kissing my mate is not a job." My mouth met hers and this was not a chaste kiss. It couldn't be. She'd pushed me too far. It was explosive, my tongue finding hers, moving in and out of her mouth as my cock would her pussy soon enough. I broke the kiss and we were panting hard. Lowering my head, I took a nipple into my mouth, sucked and laved it with my tongue, gently nipped at the tip with my teeth.

"Making your nipples hard is not a job."

I switched to the other nipple and her fingers tangled in my hair. I wanted to incite her passion, push her to the brink of coming before I took her. I wanted her as crazy as me, as wild as my beast.

I slipped my fingers between her spread thighs, coated them in her wetness, brought them to my mouth and licked them clean.

"It is not a job to taste your pussy, to make you come."

Her heavy lidded eyes flared with heat, then closed at my carnal words as I lifted her hips and then lowered her down onto my cock. She slid down over me like a glove, taking me deep. We both groaned at the pleasure. She was so hot, so wet and tight. I was big, but she took all of me. It was a perfect fit. *She* was perfect.

She began to ride me then, her hands on my shoulders for balance and forced the beast to grip her lush hips and watch her face, the glistening of her skin, the way her mouth opened as she cried out when I lifted my hips beneath her, driving deeper than I'd been before. Her head was back, her eyes closed, mouth open as she breathed hard. Her breasts bounced and swayed as she used me for her pleasure, and I couldn't fucking look away. Didn't want to stop her.

This wasn't gentle lovemaking. This was wild and carnal. Intense and powerful. I helped her to the brink and pushed her over when I slipped a finger over her slick clit and gently brushed the side of it, then over the top where the hood had pulled back.

Her fingernails dug into my shoulders as she screamed. I felt her inner walls clench down on my cock, trying to pull it in deeper. Her juices coated me completely in welcome and I used the wetness to slide in and out in a faster rhythm, drawing her orgasm out, pushing her to another. Her scent taunted the beast and I knew he would demand to taste her again soon. I would never get enough of the flavor of her arousal on my tongue, sweet like honey, yet wild and dark, appeasing my beast.

The wildness just beneath the surface, the beast growled, and I took over, holding her in place as I began to fuck up into her.

"Fuck," I murmured. She was tight, so tight she squeezed me like a vise. I was mindlessly taking her. Fucking her. Rutting like a wild animal.

She whimpered and I froze for a heartbeat in time, afraid I had hurt her. Her soft body yielded so perfectly in my arms that I had begun to lose control, to take her as I wanted. To fuck her hard, forcing her body to stretch, to accommodate my large cock.

"Don't stop!" She tugged at my hair, her hips wiggling in protest.

"I'll never fucking stop," I growled. Her eyes opened even as I thrust into her again and again. "You're mine. So fucking beautiful."

Her emerald eyes met mine. I saw the passion and desire in them, the need to come again building like storm clouds before the lightning.

"Mine. Mine. *Mine*," I rumbled with each penetrating stroke. She was my mate. I knew it. My beast knew it. The scent of her, the feel of her, the taste of her. Even the sounds of her coming. It all soothed the beast and made it howl in happiness.

As for me, the man, I needed to come. My balls had emptied onto my belly just minutes ago, but there was more seed for her. There always would be. And so I nipped at the juncture of her neck and shoulder and moved my hands to cup her bottom, to open her pussy wider. I thrust as I used my hands on her ass to pull her forward and down, onto my cock.

"Come again, love. Come all over my cock," I whispered in her ear, my voice deliberately gentle as my cock was not.

Perhaps it was the command of my words. Perhaps it was the fact that I was accepting her as my mate. Perhaps it was that I held her ass in my hands, that I held her in place, forcing her to surrender to my will.

Whatever the cause, her inner walls rippled and pulled me deeper. Her orgasm shook her body, but she did not scream. She offered no sound as I came deep inside her, filling her with my seed. I marked her, coated her with my essence.

Our orgasms put us in sync, connecting us, binding us just as the cuffs did.

She was mine. I was hers. And the beast, it was sated once more.

eek

"HOW LONG DO we have to stay?" I leaned in and whispered in Tiffani's ear. Of course, my beast detected her womanly scent and I couldn't help but kiss the side of her neck. "I won't last long with you in that dress."

"We've only been here thirty minutes," she countered, turning her head so she looked right at me, but I could see the happiness in her gaze. My compliment had pleased her.

I'd have to compliment her often.

Her green eyes were enhanced by some coloring she had added to her face. Her dress matched the color of her eyes perfectly. When she'd come out of our bedroom in her dress I'd almost come in my pants. My beast had wanted to jump on her and fuck her right in the doorway.

In fact, we'd be in bed this moment, naked and sated if she hadn't put up her hand and threatened me with death if

I messed up her up-do. I had no idea what she was talking about until she pointed to the elaborate design of her thick brown hair. It was piled atop her head in a way that had taken her and Sarah more than an hour. I had no complaints, for it perfectly framed the sensual roundness of her face and made her eyes look as if they were much larger.

She looked like a fantasy. No woman this beautiful could be real.

But she was real. And she was fucking mine. Forever. I was the luckiest bastard in the universe.

She smiled at me and took my hand in her much smaller one. The small act made something tight loosen in my chest. Thank the gods, neither of us had any shame where our connection was concerned. That slight movement, her fingers entwined with mine, was as much a public claiming as the cuffs around her wrists. But *she* was claiming *me*. Standing beside me in a room full of strangers and declaring me her own.

I was a warlord *and* a commander. I'd been in so many battles they blurred in my mind, became a constantly running stream of agony, rage, terror and death. That had been my life. Until her.

I blinked, coming out of my thoughts to find her watching me with a tender smile on her lips. I saw acceptance in her gaze. Desire. Perhaps... did I dare hope? Love? Regardless, the look was a blatant invitation and had me shifting my cock in my pants and counting the minutes until we could leave the party so I could strip her bare and sink into her.

A mated Atlan couple approached. Carvax was their name, if I remembered correctly. I shook the warrior's hand and introduced him to Tiffani, who was in turn introduced to his mate. It took all of two minutes, but when they turned away, my fake smile dropped.

"I hate these things. It was one reason I went into war and not politics."

"But I thought you wanted to... show me off." An impish smile had me wanting to spank her ass. "Those were your exact words."

"I changed my mind. I want you all to myself."

Her delighted laughter pleased me, as did the way her hand squeezed mine. "You are such a caveman."

I did not know what a caveman was, but she smiled as she said it, so it was a good thing. "That dress does the showing off all by itself."

She glanced down at her cleavage, which was too visible in her dress. "Double F in my skinny clothes."

"What does that mean? I don't understand. And I do not want a skinny mate. I like you the way you are." Unable to resist, I turned her and pulled her into my arms. Lowering my mouth to her ear, I whispered, so none of the other guests would hear. "I like you soft and round. I like to sink into your body as I bury my cock in your pussy. I like the way your breasts shift when I fuck you. I like to watch your ass sway as I spank you with one hand and fuck you with the other."

Her breathing changed and I smelled her body's response, the wet heat that flooded her pussy at my words.

"Behave, Deek." Her voice was filled with laughter.

"I told you, this damn party is going to take too long. I want you naked." I lowered my hands to her hips and pulled her closer, so she could not miss the hard welcome of my erection.

"Sarah's dress is more revealing than this," she countered.

"Sarah's cleavage is Dax's problem," I grumbled. "Resisting you is mine."

"I don't want you to resist."

My beast growled at the blatant seduction in her words. My mate was temptation in physical form. When was this fucking party going to be over?

"Commander Deek." A man cleared his throat and I reluctantly released my mate so we could both turn and greet the next who had come to congratulate us.

I tensed as I recognized Engel Steen and Tia. She was dressed in much the same manner as Tiffani, her dress a dark red and her large breasts on ample display. And yet, the beast could have been looking at a Hive soldier for all the interest it displayed in the other woman.

I shook hands with the older Atlan warlord. He was dressed in loose-fitting black and gold, his tunic and flowing pants fitting for a man of his stature, the same civilian garb I would now be expected to wear. Atlans were ever ready to fight, or defend our mates from a male in the throes of mating fever. I'd worn battle armor for so long, I felt naked in the dark gray and deep green clothing Sarah had ordered made for me so Tiffani and I would "match."

I'd thought the idea absurd at the time, but allowed the women to please themselves. I had no care for my clothing. But now, I rather enjoyed knowing that with one glance, all would know my mate was with me. Mine.

Tia cleared her throat and looked at me expectantly, tilting her head at my mate and raising her eyebrows as if I were the biggest idiot on the planet. Perhaps I was. But even as I conceded to her wishes, I was relieved to have her treat me like an annoying older brother once more, and not a potential mate.

"Tiffani, may I introduce my cousins. This is Engel Steen. He serves on the Atlan council and is in charge of all interplanetary trade."

"Nice to meet you." Tiffani held out her hand in an odd Earth custom Sarah and Tiffani had tried to explain to me. I had informed her that mated males do not enjoy watching another touch their mate. If Atlans "shook hands," as those of Earth did, warriors would get hurt.

As I expected, Engel simply stared for a moment before bowing at the waist to offer his respect, as was our custom. "My lady, it is an honor."

She grinned up at me in a flash, but I saw the defeated resignation in her eyes. I had won this argument.

Tiffani smiled at Engel and lowered her arm. "Thank you."

"This is his daughter, Tia."

I saw Tiffani stiffen at the mention of Tia, but I doubted anyone else would notice but me. She had a broad smile on her face. Tia held her hand out to my mate, whose smile turned genuine as she accepted the gesture.

"It's an honor to meet you, Tiffani. I am so glad you are here." She blushed, just a bit, but I knew Tiffani had seen the color rise in her cheeks when my mate's back stiffened and her smile turned forced once more.

"Thank you. It's nice to meet you."

Tia withdrew her hand. She stood nearly a head taller than my mate, her dark eyes round with worry as she fussed with her long dark hair, throwing it back over her shoulders as if she had nothing better to do. When Tia took a deep breath, I braced for the worst.

"Your dress is lovely," Tia offered, and I sighed with relief.

My mate's smile softened and became real. "Thank you. Yours is pretty, too."

"Since we are family now, you will have to let me show you about. While Deek is a good guide, I'm sure you'd like a female's perspective." Tia's dark eyes were sincere. "I'd really like us to be friends."

"I'd like that." Tiffani glanced up at me. "I heard that you offered to mate Deek to save him."

Tia looked apprehensive and feared answering. I didn't blame her, for it was common knowledge that Atlan mates, male and female, were quite possessive. I gave Tiffani's hand a squeeze to somehow tell her not to kill my distant cousin if she was envious.

"Yes," Tia admitted finally. "And I guess you've probably heard that Commander Deek and I were betrothed when we were five."

Tiffani's expression gave nothing away but I knew this knowledge couldn't be easy to deal with. I wrapped an arm around her waist and pulled her closer, under my arm, as Tia continued.

"I want you to know, I do love Deek. He's like a brother to me. We grew up together. But neither of us ever truly wanted to be mated, Tiffani. His beast didn't want me either. We both knew it early on. I want you to know that. When I visited him, offering myself, it was because I couldn't let him die without trying to save him. I just couldn't."

Tiffani, so stiff in my arms, relaxed, stepping forward to embrace Tia. "Thank you for trying. I understand. And I'm grateful. It's good to know that Deek has family that loves him so much."

Tiffani stepped back when Engel cleared his throat. "Yes, Deek. I am greatly relieved to know that you are well and truly mated. We were all so worried for you."

"Thank you, cousin." I'd never thought of Tia's offer as a sacrifice, as an act of love for a brother. But now, thanks to Tiffani, I understood, and the last of my anger with her faded. Her father, however, was another matter entirely. What lay between us would not be polite conversation at this party.

I looked at the woman who'd been willing to sacrifice her own chance for a true mating, her happiness, to save my life. "Thank you, Tia. I am honored."

Tia looked up at her father, nudging him with her elbow.

"Quite right," he said. "It would have been a shame to have a commander such as yourself succumb to the mating fever. It would have been a tragic waste."

Tia and Tiffani continued to chat about exploring the market, going shopping, and female things as I stared at Engel. Yes, he would think it a waste. A waste should I have succumbed to fever instead of maintaining my position as commander in the Coalition Fleet, I thought dryly. Tiffani frowned slightly, taking my hand as if she sensed my anger. I liked it very much and so did my beast. Such a simple gesture, and yet her touch soothed my irritation as nothing else could.

Engel might be my mother's cousin, but he was also an Atlan council member who had been in power for far too long. I'd been asked for favors in the past, used for my position in the Fleet by others seeking to gain, but never offered a bribe by my own family. Until Engel.

Trading Coalition weapons with primitive planets was

illegal. Engel knew this. Every first-year recruit at every level of Fleet operations knew that we didn't give ion blasters to savages. And yet Engel had wanted to do just that. I'd caught him on the *Battleship Brekk* during his visit with two crates full of blasters being loaded onto a freighter that was scheduled to deliver medical aid to a war-torn region of Xerima.

The Xerimian people were barbarians. Nearly our size, their warriors constantly battled for females and territory. The strongest took the spoils. Their planet was protected by the Coalition Fleet, but they had not been granted the rights or privileges of being a member planet. Not yet.

I'd taken the weapons and turned him in to command. But Engel had friends in very high places, and he'd been released and on his way within hours of his arrest.

The council chose to believe his lies about a mistake, an incorrect cargo manifest.

I, however, did not. And his repeated attempts to force me to mate with his daughter reeked of further manipulation. How many people would he have been able to intimidate or bribe if I had become Tia's mate? With a powerful commander as his new son?

"You were very brave, Tiffani," Tia said. "The news feeds have talked of little else since your arrival." Tia exhaled a deep breath and her words drew me from my reverie.

"News feeds? What news feeds?" Tiffani looked up at me for an explanation, which I very much did not want to give.

9

WHEN I TOOK a moment too long to answer, Tia grinned at my mate. "Didn't they tell you? You're famous."

Tiffani paled, swaying, and I frowned at Tia's antics. "Tia, stop scaring her."

"Why didn't you tell her? How many interview requests have you turned down already?"

Tiffani looked up at me with a fierce scowl, clearly growing irritated. "Well?"

With a sigh, I relented. Dax and I had discussed this problem at length in my office just hours ago. Eventually, I was going to be forced to concede. My people wanted to know Tiffani, loved her for saving my life. I was a selfish bastard, keeping her all to myself. The world would understand that my mating fever would take some time to soothe. But I was running out of ways to keep the media away.

Before long, the curious would be knocking on our door. "Twenty-two."

"Oh, my God." Tiffani's eyes were round with surprise. "I'm a waitress from Milwaukee. I'm really not that interesting."

I sighed. "That was just yesterday."

Tia crossed her arms with a snort. "You can't hide her in your bedroom forever, *Commander*."

Tiffani started to laugh, but still blushed furiously, and reached out to place her hand on Tia's forearm. "Thanks for the warning."

Tia looked confused by the touch—my mate was very into touching—but then grinned. "Well, we are family now. And we women need to stick together."

"That reminds me," Engel said.

We all looked to him as he pulled something from his pants pocket. It was a small pouch, black with a gold pull string.

"This is for you." Engel held the pouch out to Tiffani, but looked at me. "A peace offering and apology. Welcome to the family, Tiffani."

Tiffani took the proffered bag and opened it, letting the contents fall into her small hand. "It's beautiful. Thank you."

The clenched muscles in my neck and jaw relaxed as I saw the necklace. Links of gold entwined with graphite designs engraved with the symbols of our family line. This was the gift I had refused while in the prison cell. But this time, Tia did not offer it to me, but to my mate.

As if reading my mind, Engel looked up at me. "Since Tiffani is your mate and this is a family heirloom, we felt she should have it."

I glanced at Tia to see if she agreed. She nodded. "It will look great with that dress, Tiffani."

Tiffani held up the gift, offering it to me. "Will you help?"

"Of course." I would always help her, be the task large or small.

I lifted the necklace from her palm and ran my fingers along the familiar metal links. I remembered it well. "I used to sit on my grandmother's lap and play with this when I was very small. I liked the way the lights reflected off the gold."

"Perhaps our son will do the same someday." Tiffani offered the vision and turned her back to me. Opening the clasp, I draped the costly jewelry around her neck, leaning to place a kiss on her shoulder. Now I could not stop envisioning my son on Tiffani's lap, his chubby little hand reaching for the golden links. Truly grateful and humbled by the gift, I released her to face Engel.

"Very generous, Councilor. And it looks perfect on my mate. Thank you."

Tiffani put her hand on the cool links then offered her thanks as well.

Another couple came to stand beside Engel. He glanced at them and nodded. "You have more guests to greet. We won't keep you."

Engel nodded and took Tia by the arm, steering her toward the refreshment table as Tiffani's words chased them. "Call me, or whatever. I want to go shopping soon!"

"You got it!" Tia's grin was filled with joy and I let my anger with Engel go. He was an old man playing an age-old game. I'd done my duty. Turned him in. It was time for me to let go of the past and enjoy my future with my new mate.

.   .   .

TIFFANI

WHILE I WAS ENJOYING the party, I had the same thoughts as Deek. I wanted to leave and get my mate naked. I was used to seeing him either in his armor or naked, but in fancy clothes, in what I thought of as an Atlan tuxedo, he looked... incredible. Edible.

And yet I had been the one to promise Sarah we would remain until the final guests were gone. Therefore, I had to restrain myself and resist my mate until the very end. If I even mentioned an interest in leaving, or even in just finding a quiet room somewhere and having an Atlan quickie, Deek would have tossed me over his shoulder and shouted out a goodbye. And so I just reveled in his constant attention, his constant touch, and enjoyed something I'd never had before—a smoking-hot man's undivided attention.

It was because he was always touching me that I sensed a change in him before anyone else. His hand became hot to the touch, as if he were feverish. He became restless. His eyes, which had been calm and content all evening, now darted at every man who passed, searched every shadow for danger. He moved closer to me, hovering to the point of being ridiculous.

I appreciated the fact that he was protective, but this was a bit extreme. It was literally as if he couldn't be more than a few inches from me. He held me around the waist or shoulder at all times, forcing our bodies to touch constantly.

He spoke less to the guests. Within a matter of minutes he was reduced to single-word replies. Grunts, even.

I looked up at him and noticed he was sweating and tugging at the collar of his shirt. His skin was flushed and his eyes were dark, so much darker than I'd seen. Except when—

Oh, shit.

"Deek," I said, tugging on his hand. "What's wrong?"

The couple standing with us noticed the change in him and retreated quickly, their eyes wary as they whispered to each other.

"Fever," he growled.

"Let's get you out of here," I murmured, tugging on his hand to steer him out of the room. Fortunately, he allowed me to pull him along.

"Commander."

Engel Steen stepped in front of us, blocking our way. His gaze shifted between me and Deek, then settled on my mate with a frown.

"Is there a problem?" he asked.

Shaking my head and offering him a fake smile, I tried to move around him, pulling a very big Atlan commander in the throes of mating fever behind me. "No, no problem. We're just very eager to... um, to be alone."

Engel put a hand on my shoulder to stop me. "You have yet to meet the other councilor that just arrived. He will be very disappointed to have—"

Deek's beast growled at the man's touch and I instantly remembered that mated Atlans had a no-touching rule. Pulling back from Engel's hand, I broke the councilor's contact with my shoulder, but it was too late. Deek's growl turned into an all-out roar, which practically shook the walls of Dax and Sarah's house.

Everyone quieted and turned toward us. Before my eyes, Deek changed. His teeth became more pronounced, more like fangs. His chest and shoulders bulged, his arms nearly doubling in size as the muscle fibers expanded into the beast's fighting mode. He grew nearly a foot taller, his spine elongating as he rose to tower above everyone in the room.

"Deek. Calm down." I couldn't help but stare at him, for while he'd been in beast mode at the jail cell, I'd never watched the actual transformation before. It was like watching an old episode of *The Incredible Hulk* on TV, but at least his clothes didn't rip and fall into tatters. Seemed the Atlans made their clothes with beast mode in mind.

"He's still got the fever," Engel said, wide-eyed, as he put his hands out before him and backed away.

Deek was panting and only my hand on his chest kept him from jumping Engel.

"No touch," Deek said, his voice that dark, deep rumble I remembered from before we mated.

"Step away, Engel. You shouldn't have touched me," I told him.

Engel took another step back. "I regret that now, but that is not what we should be focusing on."

Dax and Sarah came to stand next to most of the party-goers, who were gathering. The male warriors shoved their mates behind them, just in case. In moments we were completely surrounded by over a dozen warriors whose sharp gazes and tense stance let me know they were ready to take Deek down at any moment.

Oh, shit. I turned to Deek, touched his cheek. "Deek, baby, calm down."

He wouldn't even look at me as Engel stepped forward again. It looked as if he might be coming closer, which made me wince and Deek roar.

Engel froze and turned to Dax. "Commander Deek's mating fever has returned. You must summon the guards at once."

I wanted to punch Engel for stating the obvious about Deek's condition, but I wanted to kick him in the balls for daring suggest they drag my mate back to prison.

I whirled on Dax. "Don't you dare. Just help me get him out of here. I'm his mate. He'll be fine."

"No touch," Deek repeated, his eyes focused on Engel with laser sharpness, his hands tightly clenched into fists. "Mate."

"Mate?" Engel said, voice incredulous, and a bit too loud for my liking. "She can't be your mate. Look at you."

Engel lifted his arm and waved it through the air. Everyone turned to look at Deek, whose eyes were nearly bulging from his head as he processed Engel's claim. His breathing was rushed and ragged, as if he had just been in battle.

"Don't listen to him, Deek. I'm your mate. I don't care what he says."

Apparently, when being challenged by another warlord, the woman being argued over became invisible, because Deek picked me up and set me down behind him, out of the way.

"Mate!" Deek shouted.

"She can't be your mate, Commander. Or you wouldn't be losing control." His tone wasn't loud or argumentative, it was patronizing, as if he were explaining two plus two to a five-year-old.

"Don't mansplain your bullshit to me, Engel." I shoved around Deek's giant torso to scowl at Engel. Stupid ass. If he'd just let me get Deek out of here in the first place, none of this would be happening. God help me, I upgraded kicking him in the nuts to shoving a boot up his ass.

"I am simply stating the obvious, dear. You aren't his mate. You can't be."

Before I could even scream at Deek to stop, he'd lunged at Engel. The older man was knocked to the floor and Deek literally jumped on top of him, arm raised to punch him. Or worse.

I screamed, but it was mixed in with the shouts of surprise from the others.

Dax stepped forward and grabbed Deek's raised arm. But Deek was enraged, and it took four more of the waiting warriors to restrain him.

"Deek!" he shouted, using all of his Atlan warlord strength to tug him off Engel Steen. "Get control of your beast. Now!" Dax turned to me. "Tiffani! Get over here and help us!"

I ran to Deek's side and placed my hand on the sides of his waist, wrapping my arms around him so he would know I was near. It seemed to help, but I knew if the others released him, he would once more lunge for the councilor.

"Gods, that man has lost control. The fever has made him a madman!" Engel was lying on his back on the floor, his arms raised to defend himself. A small cut was on his brow, but I had no idea how he'd gotten it since Deek hadn't actually punched him.

Tia dropped to her knees beside her father, worry on her face, but looked to Deek with a mixture of horror and sadness. "This can't be happening." Her gaze drifted to mine and I stared her down, daring her to repeat the nonsense about Deek not being mine. He was mine. Mine!

Dax stood between Deek and Engel, pushing Deek back with all of his strength.

I didn't care about Engel, only for Deek. The beast seethed and raged. Sweat dripped from his face and his eyes. God, his eyes were wild. My Deek was no longer there, only the beast.

"Deek," Dax said. "Commander."

Deek growled at the last, trying to break past the beast to find his voice.

"Commander," Dax repeated. "Stand down."

"Mine," Deek growled. "Mate."

The beast did not like the idea of me not actually being his mate. While it made me feel good to know the beast was so adamant about me belonging to him, I knew this little interlude meant trouble for Deek.

"That warlord has lost all control!" Engel shouted. "You saw him. You saw what he did."

He spoke to the guests and they nodded their heads, watching as Deek still fought for control over his beast. The mating fever was known by all and easily recognized. Hell, I'd been on Atlan a week and I knew what it looked like.

The guests started to murmur.

The fever returned.

Their mating wasn't true.

Obviously, the alien woman was not his real mate.

He needs to be put away.

How sad. He's going to be executed.

10

Executed?

The word sliced through my heart. How dare these strangers question what we shared? They knew nothing about our match, of what we were to each other.

But I couldn't deny the fever had returned.

"Call the guards," Engel said as he stood, legs shaky. "Tia, hurry and summon the guards. He must be put away. He's a danger to himself and everyone in this room." Engel's gaze turned to me and he softened his voice. "Including you, dear. I'm so sorry."

Dax was murmuring to Deek, but I couldn't hear what he was saying. I moved to stand before my mate, hoping both my touch and the sight of me safe and whole would soothe him. I couldn't fuck him in front of these guests, but at this point it wouldn't matter. We'd fucked like rabbits for days and yet the fever had returned to claim him.

As I touched Deek's hot skin, Engel's somber gaze watched every move I made. He didn't believe I was Deek's one true mate. I could see it in his eyes. I wore the cuffs, which were supposed to be designed to help the males control their beasts. I had no idea how the circuitry worked on the warlords who wore them, but I'd tested the perimeter of my own cuffs two days ago and had collapsed in agony when I'd gone too far from his side. He'd argued with me, not wanting me to suffer, but I'd been adamant about testing them.

And wished I had listened to him. It was like being struck by a Taser.

So, I'd stayed at his side, content to do so, and not because it fucking hurt otherwise. I'd allowed him take my body whenever he wanted. I'd given him everything. *Everything.* And it wasn't enough.

I knew that I was no good for him now. I could offer him nothing. No matter how badly I wanted more, I wasn't the right woman for him. Perhaps Engel was right. Other than the cuffs, we had no proof of a mating bond between us, whatever that even meant. I'd been told at least a half-dozen times that an Atlan's mate was the only one who could control her mate's beast. The only person in the universe an Atlan in beast mode would listen to.

Well, I'd failed at that, too.

The guards came through the doors with their ion blasters raised.

"Put those fucking weapons away," Dax shouted at them. "He's a commander in fever, not a criminal."

"He knocked me down. Everyone saw it. I'm sorry, Dax. I

know he's your friend, but he's dangerous," Engel countered.

Engel looked to me as he said the last as Deek was put in restraints above his forearms.

The guards started to lead him toward the door.

"Mate," Deek growled.

"She must go with him," Dax insisted.

I didn't want to leave Deek's side, but I had not expected Dax to say I had to go to the jail with him. I could do nothing to help him control his beast. I had no idea why he'd responded to me the first time, although he hadn't been as out of control as he was now.

"He will hurt her!" Tia countered, coming to stand beside me. "You can stay with me," she said, looking at me with sad eyes.

"She must go," Dax repeated. "They are cuffed."

The cuffs. That was why I had to go. Not because I was Deek's mate, but because the pain would be too great for us to be apart.

"I will go," I said, lifting my chin and moving to stand behind the guards. This was one of the most mortifying—and heartbreaking—moments of my life. Everyone knew that I failed, that I wasn't enough for a commander. That I wasn't his mate. I'd failed.

"I will stay with him," I murmured past a lump in my throat. I would not cry.

"In jail?" Tia countered.

"I've been there before. I am not afraid." And the truth of it was, I couldn't bear to leave his side.

"He won't be there long, I'm afraid." Engel sidled up to his daughter's shoulder with a resigned sigh. "In cases like this, the execution order will most likely be reinstated and carried out swiftly."

It was like he'd stabbed me in the gut with a dagger. "How long does he have?" I wasn't afraid of the jail. I was afraid of what was going to happen to Deek. It was because of me that he was in trouble again. I didn't mate him correctly. His seed didn't take, or bond, or whatever. I wasn't enough for him. I hadn't pleased his beast enough.

"Hours." Dax answered my question. Tears gathered in my eyes, but I didn't have time for a mental breakdown. They were leading my mate out into a large vehicle of some kind for transport to the prison.

Deek was going to die. This time, I wasn't going to be able to save him.

Dax escorted me to the prison transport and I was assisted into the back by one of the guards. I didn't look him in the eye. I didn't look anyone in the eye. I didn't want to see pity there, or judgment. And if I saw even a hint of sympathy, I was going to lose it. Tears. Big, fat ugly cry.

I loved my mate. I loved him. He was big and brutish and all fucking man. He'd made me feel beautiful and worthy and wanted for the first time in my life, and I didn't want to give that up. I loved the way he fucked me up against the wall. The way he shouldered his head between my thighs and licked and sucked until I screamed his name. I loved the way he stared at my body, at my breasts and belly, as if I were a delicious treat. I loved being with him.

And now, because of me, he was going to die.

I sat in silence for the short ride to the prison, where I was helped from the vehicle with Deek close behind. He was still panting, his skin flushed and his eyes darting around like every shadow held an enemy.

With a sigh, I followed the small column of warriors who walked us down the long, cream-colored hallway and back to the same cell he'd been in when I arrived. Block 4. Cell 11.

I walked into the cell and straight to the bed where I climbed up onto the mattress and curled into a ball on my side.

If Deek came for me, I would try my best to soothe him. But even if I fucked his brains out, sucked his cock, made him grunt and growl and say my name with a reverence I'd never heard from anyone else, it wouldn't matter.

I could fuck him silly, but I couldn't control his beast. Only his true mate could do that. Only his true mate could save him. And if that female appeared now and took him, mating with him, easing his beast, my heart would break into a million tiny little pieces. He was supposed to be mine. Forever.

I heard the force field they called a grav-wall turn on, but I ignored it. I kept my back to Deek as he paced and growled. I couldn't bear to look at him. It hurt too much.

Tears slid in silent streams from my eyelids and into the bedding. Deek didn't speak to me, but after a while he climbed onto the bed and lay down beside me, pulling me into his arms. My back pressed to his overheated chest, his monster-sized arms wrapped around me. I was mentally exhausted, but refused to sleep.

If we only had a few hours left, I didn't want to waste them oblivious to the warmth of my Deek's arms around me.

The heavy golden chain around my neck suddenly felt like a curse, like a taunt, a tease. That gold represented forever, my place in Deek's family.

And now it meant nothing but lost dreams and regret.

I MUST HAVE DRIFTED OFF, for when I next opened my eyes, it was to hear women's voices. I thought it odd, then remembered what Sarah had told me about Atlan women parading through this prison they called a containment facility to offer the Atlan males one last chance at finding a mate. Their presence filled me with rage as I considered the possibility that one of them might be a match for Deek.

He was mine.

Except he wasn't. Or we wouldn't be here.

Lifting my hand, I ran the sensitive tips of my fingers along the gold and dark gray carved links around my neck. They were a symbol of my claim on Deek, my status as his matched mate. They were a visible declaration of my hold over him, of my ability to control his beast.

Except, I'd failed.

Perhaps one of those women would be more beautiful, more desirable. Perhaps one of them could save him.

Unfortunately, there was only one way to determine if any of them coming through the facility could offer solace to the males condemned to die. That, of course, included fucking to see if the beast was compatible.

I shifted beneath the heavy arm thrown over my waist and scooted from the bed as quietly as I could. When Deek stirred, I murmured for him to go back to sleep. Which, to my extreme shock, he did.

He never slept this deeply. Every night, all I need do was shift beneath the covers and he was instantly on alert. He'd claimed it was due to too many combat missions, too much time spent on the front, where the extra few seconds it took to wake could cost you your life.

But here, now? He barely lifted his head, the blink of his eyelids slow, as if they were heavy.

Shaking my head, I walked to the grav-wall to find several Atlan females slowly moving from cell to cell down the corridor, peeking into each one and seeing the prisoners, deciding if one was appealing.

One female stopped in front of me. I inspected her on the other side of the shimmering force field and tried not to show how much I was hurting. She was tall, like all Atlan females, almost a foot taller than me. Her hair was a light summer blond with shimmering highlights and the mass fell past her waist. Her breasts were larger than mine, but her waist was trim and defined, and the muscles in her arms and legs would have qualified her for a bodybuilder competition back home.

And, as if that weren't enough, she was gorgeous. Pale blue eyes and pink lips. She looked like a giant edition fashion model.

No fucking way I could compete with that.

"Hello. I'm Seranda."

Even her voice was soft and lilting, beautiful.

I nodded in reply.

"I am here to help," she said, looking around me to Deek.

My pulse pounded, but I tried to keep the panic from rising. "Help with what?"

"I heard of you on the media and I'm sorry things didn't work out between you and Deek. He's a fierce and highly respected warrior." Her voice held more than a little awe as her gaze left me and traveled to the bed behind me, where my mate, my Deek, still slept. Her gaze was more than interested, and I fought back the scowl I knew would form between my brows. I didn't have a right to that scowl. I didn't have the right to Deek. Not anymore.

When her gaze returned to me, there was pity in her pale blue eyes. "He is gorgeous, Tiffani Wilson of Earth. I'd like to help you save him."

I arched my brow at what she was insinuating. "You... you want to fuck him and see if his beast likes you."

"Likes me?" She shrugged her perfect shoulders. "His beast needs to recognize me as his mate."

I pursed my lips. "Yes, I'm well aware of that. What if it doesn't work?"

"Then I will have tried, won't I? And you will have lost nothing. His execution was announced not long ago."

My heart skipped a beat, agony like a pickax buried in my chest. "When?"

"Today. He has eight hours."

I wanted to poke her eyes out, but it wouldn't make a difference. I wasn't Deek's mate. I had no sway over him, no say in who he should be with. I was nothing to him now.

But I loved him. He was a gentle, caring lover one moment, a demanding animal the next. He always took care of me, made me feel like I was his sun and stars, like he'd do anything for me. Die to protect me. He made me feel wanted. Beautiful. Whole. He made me feel whole.

"What if it doesn't work?"

"Then he dies." She shrugged. "But at least you'll know you tried to save him. If you say no, your selfish jealousy will mean his death."

Wow. The claws had come out. The bitch was insinuating that I would be killing him if I didn't let her come into the cell and fuck him, try to calm his beast. I imagined him with her and nearly threw up all over my pretty slippers. Deek was good in bed, no, incredible, but it was our connection that made it that way. We'd connected, perhaps not as mates, but in a way I never had before, with any other man. And that was why my heart was broken. I loved him. I'd given him more than my body. I'd given him my heart. My soul.

And now I had to watch him die.

Or, I could let him see if any of these Atlan females, including Seranda, were his real mate. If I was not his true mate, remaining within the cell with him was only guaranteeing his execution.

Instead of helping him, comforting him, I was condemning him.

I looked down at the cuffs about my wrists. I'd grown accustomed to the heavy weight of them, for they were a constant reminder of my connection to Deek.

Now though, they were like shackles, keeping him connected to me when I wasn't the one for him. When my presence would mean his death.

I looked to Seranda. I was just like her. Yes, heavier, less pretty, and definitely not Atlan. I'd been brought to the cell by Dax and Sarah in the hopes that I would be a match, that my body would soothe the beast. The Bride Program had assured me of the match, but it was a computer program and certainly not infallible.

I was the same as Seranda, only less. A failure. The cuffs didn't belong to me.

Deek didn't belong to me.

I fiddled with a cuff, trying to figure out how to open it. Frustrated, I tugged and pulled at it, tears streaming down my face. I hadn't cried before now, but the cuffs were all that was left between us. And now I was getting rid of them. Of us.

Finally, I found the strange indentation that released the latch and the cuff gave way. The second was much easier to remove. I placed them on the floor at my feet and wiped the tears from my cheeks.

"Call the guard, Seranda. Have the grav-wall dropped. Try to save him."

She nodded, her expression grave, not victorious. She truly was sorry for me. I believed that she respected and admired Deek, that she truly wanted him, wanted to save him. And that made the whole damn thing hurt even more.

I waited for the grav-wall to be deactivated, then walked down the corridor. I glanced over my shoulder and saw Seranda tug the straps of her dress off her shoulders. I caught a glimpse of her perfect breasts before she stepped into Deek's cell. I could envision her, naked and perfect, waking Deek from his sleep.

I turned and fled, knowing I belonged there no longer.

11

I WAS EXHAUSTED, so weary that I didn't wish to wake up. But Tiffani was in my arms. No, she was on top of me, kissing my neck and slowly unbuttoning my shirt. I made a sound of satisfaction, but my beast prowled, nudged me. It had prodded me to wake. Why? Why would my beast not settle and preen beneath Tiffani's attentions?

"You're so big."

I stilled at the voice while my beast practically howled with rage.

The scent of turins, the seasonal flower that appeared at the beginning of the warm months on Atlan, was cloying.

I opened my eyes and saw pale hair. Someone, not Tiffani, was on top of me, sucking at the skin on my neck.

Finally wide awake, the beast growled and my chest rumbled. Grabbing the female about the waist—her bare waist—I lifted her up and off me, placed her on her feet to stand beside the bed.

I leapt to my feet and walked across the cell to get as much distance from her as possible. Raking my hand through my hair, I saw then that she was completely naked. She didn't hide her body, but rolled her shoulders back and lifted her chin so I could see all of her... assets.

"Commander, I'm here to serve you," she said, and there was no mistaking the manner in which she intended to *serve*.

"Where the hell is Tiffani?"

The cell wasn't big. It wasn't as if she were hiding beneath the bed.

"Gone." She seductively ran her hands down her sides and over her hips, then bringing them back up her flat belly to stroke over her breasts. I watched as her nipples tightened. Any Atlan male would be aroused by her, but I was disgusted by her flaunting. She wasn't what I wanted. I wanted brown hair and green eyes. I wanted soft and round, a woman to sink into, to dominate, not wrestle with in bed.

"Gone?" I asked as I went back to the bed, ripped the sheet off it and tossed it at her. "Cover yourself, female."

"My name is Seranda, and I am here to soothe your beast," she repeated.

She fumbled with the sheet and held it up in front of herself. Most of her body was hidden, but it still offered tantalizing glimpses of the curve of her hip and a bare shoulder.

Her words gave me pause. My beast was prowling and growling because an unmated female was in my cell. Naked. On top of me and licking my neck. It wasn't riled because of the fever. That affliction was gone.

For now.

"My beast needs Tiffani."

"Your beast needs a mate, or you die." She tilted her head, annoyance making her purse her lips. "In less than eight hours."

She was beautiful, her body lush and perfect... for someone else. She was also a bitch.

"Tiffani is my mate," I ground out through clenched teeth.

Seranda slowly shook her head and pointed to the cuffs that were on the floor by the grav-wall. "No, she's not. Who do you think let me in? She left you, Commander."

Crossing to them, I picked them up, stunned.

The cuffs were cool to the touch. Empty. "Fuck."

Spinning on my heel, I faced the Atlan female. Her name was already forgotten. If she left the cell, her face, her body, would be forgotten. My beast wanted Tiffani and no other. She was my mate. I knew it. My beast knew it.

But I still was afflicted with the fever. It made no sense to me. To my beast, it was simple. It wanted Tiffani.

"Get out," I growled.

"I am here to soothe you."

"I do not want to be soothed. I want Tiffani."

"I could be your mate," she countered.

My beast snarled and snapped at the idea.

"No."

"You will die," she said again. "You should at least try, Commander. Touch me. Let me touch you. Give me a chance to save you."

She took one step toward me, but I held up my hand.

"No."

"She took the cuffs off to save you."

I looked at her then to see if she was lying. "What?"

"She doesn't want you to die. For an alien, she is... nice. She took the cuffs off so that you could fuck me. To see if your beast would be soothed, your mating fever gone."

"She *wanted* me to fuck you?"

For the first time, the Atlan female looked less than confident. "No, I think she wanted to tear my eyes out. But she knew she wasn't your mate, that she couldn't save you, couldn't control your beast. She was crying, Commander, but very brave. She left to save your life. Don't let her sacrifice be in vain."

I wasn't sure if I wanted to take Tiffani over my knee and spank her until her ass was too red and sore to sit for a week or pull her into my arms and kiss her senseless for being so selfless, so brave, so damn stubborn.

Either way, it didn't matter. She was gone and I was stuck with an Atlan female who wanted to fuck my beast. My cock was flaccid in my pants. Neither man nor beast was interested.

Fuck. I was going to die.

TIFFANI

SARAH AND DAX were kind enough to allow me back in their home. I had nowhere else to go on Atlan. Deek's house was no longer mine. While I was told I was quite famous for bravely entering Deek's jail cell and saving him by mating with him, I was now infamous for the entire thing failing miserably.

I had no idea how to turn on the Atlan version of a TV, but I didn't want to. Whatever was being said about me was nothing I wanted to hear.

With no friends and no prospects, I had to wonder what would happen to me. Per the Bride's Program rules, if a match didn't work for whatever reason, I could find another. I couldn't leave Atlan and return to Earth per Bride Program rules, but I could accept the next mate that was an acceptable match. But the match wouldn't be as strong, it wouldn't be the same. It wouldn't be Deek.

But it looked as if I had no other choice. While Deek would be fucking every willing Atlan female to find a mate and save his life, I would have to be matched to someone new. I'd either have to live nearby and watch him with some other female, or worse, live knowing Deek had been executed.

I hated the thought of him touching someone else, loving someone else. But I loved him too much to let him die. Either way, I lost. I cried myself to sleep, at least fitfully. I'd walked away. I'd been strong enough to do that. What girl could do anything else?

I couldn't settle at first because I was crying so much. My nose was so stuffy I could barely breathe and I couldn't relax knowing Deek was probably fucking Seranda six ways to Sunday. But then I became restless for a different reason. I couldn't keep my legs still, couldn't get comfortable. I felt like I'd had four cups of high-octane coffee and while my brain was exhausted from overthinking, my body was wound up.

I got out of bed and started to pace. My skin tingled and I rubbed it, as if the cool air in the guest bedroom was irritating. The light became too bright, so I turned it down. My mouth became dry and I was thirsty. So very thirsty. I ran to the kitchen and remembered how Sarah had retrieved a glass and filled it with water.

I guzzled it down, filled it again.

I imagined Deek fucking that other woman, pinning her to the wall as his beast thrust into her without mercy. I imagined the intense look of pleasure I'd often seen on his face, the darkening of his eyes. His growl.

God, that sound. My pussy clenched and grew wet, which just made me angrier. Tears streaked from my eyes as I drank a third glass of water. My breasts tingled now, and I imagined Deek's mouth on them, sucking them deeply into his mouth, kneading their heavy weight until I moaned and begged him to take me.

Seranda. She had his mouth on her breasts now, on her skin, her hot, wet...

Nope. Couldn't go there. I needed a distraction. Something to do.

Glancing around the kitchen frantically, my heart racing like a hummingbird's, I spotted my salvation. A speck of dirt on the white tile floor. That couldn't stay there. It looked wrong and it made the floor dirty, probably teeming with germs.

Frantic, I found a cloth and poured water from my cup on it. Dropping to my hands and knees, I began to scrub Sarah's floor, first removing that spot of dirt, then moving farther and farther across the hard floor. My knees hurt like hell, but I didn't care. Anything was better than focusing on the feeling of Deek's cock inside me...

"Tiffani!" Sarah called.

I glanced up at her with wide eyes. "What?"

"What are you doing?"

Dax came up behind her, put his hands on her shoulders and looked at me with a frown.

"What? There was a spot of dirt on the floor and it needed to be cleaned. The whole floor needed to be cleaned. There are germs. Bugs. Everywhere." I returned my attention to the task at hand. Sweat ran down my forehead, dripping on the marbled tile. With a gasp, I wiped it away immediately, but another followed the first. Then a third. After that, I scrubbed and scrubbed, not sure if I was wiping away sweat or tears.

Seranda had his cock now, too. She had everything.

Sarah's eyes widened. "Are you okay?"

I shook my head. "He's fucking Seranda right now. This very second. I can feel it."

Dax's soft rumble of disapproval did not help my mood. "You should not have left him."

"They're going to kill him. Kill him. Kill him." God, was it eight hundred degrees in here, or was it just me? Annoyed with my robe, I ripped it from my body and tossed it onto the floor. The skin of my arms and hands was a bright pink.

Hah! I knew it. Too damn hot.

Sarah crept forward as I returned attention to my scrubbing. "How much wine did you drink?" she asked.

"Wine? No wine. I was thirsty. I had water. I need more water." I stood, filling the cup for a fourth time. I drained it all at once, pouring a small amount on my chest and neck. So fucking hot. "It's hot in here. Don't you aliens have air conditioning?"

Sarah glanced at Dax, then back at me. "The temperature is fine, Tiff. Why don't you get up? I'll take you back to your room."

"No. I have to clean the floor."

"You hate to clean," she prompted me. I did. Ever since the restaurant, I didn't like to do it. Deek had servants to clean and so did Dax. But here I was on the floor, scrubbing it. Why?

I stood slowly, looked down at the cloth in my hand, saw that my hands were both shaking. Forget the four cups of high-octane coffee. This felt like half a case of Red Bull. My heart was racing so fast beneath my ribcage that it actually started to hurt.

"There's something wrong with me."

12

Tiffani

SARAH APPROACHED THEN, took the cloth from me, tossed it onto the table. She looked at me closely, took my chin in her hand.

"Did you take something?"

"Take?" I asked rubbing my hands over my bare arms, itchy. Tense. My heart was going too fast. Too fast. I needed ice water. More water. Did they have ice cream on this stupid planet? Chocolate chocolate chunk? Something. "Is it hot in here?"

"Tiffani, what did you take?"

"Take? What do you mean? Like an aspirin?"

Sarah nodded.

"Nothing."

Sarah looked over her shoulder at Dax.

"Are you sure?" Dax asked.

"Yes. I was in bed crying, and then I started to feel weird. God, there's something wrong with me. I can't settle down and my skin feels creepy, like ants are crawling all over me."

I shivered, tugging at the seams of my dress, twitching. Ants? Maybe. Did they have little tiny spiders on this planet? Maybe it was spiders. I shivered, rubbing at my skin as if something truly was crawling all over me. But I saw nothing. I was so confused. "Do you have spiders? And why am I scrubbing your floor?"

I looked down at the clean white tile. I'd seen one tiny little speck of dirt and freaked. I'd tackled piles of greasy pans and cleaned restaurant fryers. This was nothing. Nothing. A speck of dirt?

Was it moving? Was it a spider?

I stepped back, looking for something to crush it with from far away. Did they have cast iron here? A broom? A broom might work.

My empty glass caught my eye.

God, I was still thirsty. "I'm thirsty, Sarah. I'm sorry. Can I have another glass of water?"

"How many have you had?"

I had to think for a minute. "I don't know. Three. No, four. I think I've been roofied."

Sarah didn't roll her eyes at me. "Well, roofies would put you to sleep, not make you hyper."

"Right." Shit. I knew that. I'd seen it happen once at the restaurant. What was wrong with me?

"What is roofies?" Dax asked.

"It's a drug that puts a person to sleep. Out cold, and when they wake up, they don't remember anything that happened. It's used on Earth, at least where Tiffani and I lived, as a drug to rape women."

"Gods," Dax growled. "Has anyone touched you, Tiffani?"

I shook my head. "Only Deek, but that was before his fever hit at the party. After that, he refused to touch me. Although we did share a bed in the cell. He wrapped his arms around me and I fell asleep. But that's it."

"Did you eat or drink anything anyone strange gave you at the party?" Sarah asked.

"Only from Deek."

Dax went to a wall unit, took out an odd-looking black object with a strange coil at the top and returned to me. He pressed a button on it somewhere and a blue light lit the coils.

I frowned and tilted my head back away from it.

"It's okay," Sarah said. "It's a ReGen wand, remember? Got rid of your headache. It heals wounds and stuff."

Right. My headache from the NPU when I'd first arrived. That felt like a hundred years ago.

I just stood there with a funny look on my face as Dax waved the wand in front of my head, then lower, working his way all the way down my body, then back up again.

"Well?" he asked, when done. "Feel better?"

I shook my head. "No. I don't feel any different."

"What *do* you feel like?" Sarah asked.

"My heart is racing and I'm hot. Every spot I see in the floor is making me crazy. I'm thirsty. My skin is tingling. Look, it's pink." I held out my arm for Sarah's inspection, but Dax looked me over as well as I continued. "And I'm..." Shit, I couldn't say it.

"Horny as hell?" Sarah finished for me.

I blushed then, but Sarah wasn't laughing. "Yes. I can't stop thinking about Deek, about... what we did together."

Dax studied me. "If it wasn't something you ate, then who did you come in contact with?"

I thought about the party, began pacing the kitchen, letting some of my restless energy bleed off.

"I came in contact with everyone at the party, but no one touches here. You guys are all too macho or whatever. So crazy. You guys are crazy, you know that?" God, Deek was so possessive, so growly when another man even looked at me, and I loved it! Loved the feeling of being cherished. Desired. Wanted.

And now, he wanted Seranda.

Dax growled. "Yes, no one touches another's mate."

I thought back. "Engel does. He touched me. He made Deek go crazy. He's a jerk. I don't like him."

I blurted the words and immediately felt contrite. He was Deek's cousin. Family. I shouldn't disrespect Deek's family.

"I'm sorry. I shouldn't have said that." I looked at Sarah, pleading. "Please don't tell Deek I said that." Not that it would matter, because he wasn't mine anymore.

I moaned in pain and turned away.

"Tiffani, it's okay. We won't tell him," Sarah whispered.

Needing to believe her, I turned my head and watched her nod solemnly at me. Good. She wouldn't tell. The relief was immense and instant and I felt like a three-year-old who'd just been handed a lollipop.

Dax tilted his head, watching me. "What did you mean about Engel touching you?"

It was hard to think, but not to recall the creepy feeling of Engel's hand. "I put my hand out for Engel Steen, Deek's cousin, uncle, whatever he is. He didn't take it, but I shook Tia's hand. I guess she knew it was an Earth thing."

"Tia?" Sarah asked. "Why would she do this to you?"

"She wouldn't," Dax said. "But we were talking about Engel Steen, Tiffani. Try to remember. Did he touch you?"

I shook my head slowly as I continued to pace. "The only time was when Engel touched me at the end. I didn't like it, but Deek was already crazy with his fever. Remember, Engel touching me was what got him all fired up and out of control."

I stopped moving and clenched my hands into fists, furious all over again about Deek.

"Are you sure there's not anything else?" Sarah asked. "Close your eyes and think."

I did as she asked, working my way through the timeline of the party. "The first guests arrived and Deek actually reminded me that Atlans didn't shake hands, but bowed in greeting, so I was thinking of that at the beginning. There was that ridiculously tall guy, remember him?" I asked, keeping my eyes closed.

Sarah laughed. "Yeah, he could have played basketball, huh?"

"After he left, Engel and Tia came. That was when I shook her hand. Engel gave me Deek's family necklace."

My eyes popped open and I touched the links that still rested at the base of my neck.

"Oh, God," I said, tugging at the clasp at the back, trying to take it off. "It's the necklace. Of course, it's the fucking necklace."

"What are you talking about?" Sarah said, coming over to help.

"Don't touch it!" Dax yelled, grabbing Sarah. He took a breath when she jumped away from me. "I'm sorry for yelling, but if it is the necklace that's making her act this way, I don't want you touching it."

He leaned down and kissed Sarah's brow while I fiddled with the clasp, then got it off. I held it in the air as if it were a dead snake.

Dax retrieved a small wooden box and I dropped it inside. He placed it on the table and picked up the ReGen wand. "I'm going to change the settings. If you've got poison in your system, this will analyze the chemical and program your cells to begin to produce an antidote." The blue coils turned a strange shade of orange as he waved it over me again.

Within a couple of minutes, I started to feel better. My skin stopped being so sensitive, my breathing slowed and I didn't feel as on edge. I no longer felt as if I wanted to run a marathon or scrub their house.

I took a deep breath, then another. "Holy shit. That's so much better."

Dax looked at the ReGen wand, growled. "I fucking knew it."

"What?" Sarah and I asked in unison.

"It's Rush."

"What's Rush?" I glanced down at the box and the necklace most likely coated in the stuff.

"It's been banned for decades. Highly illegal. It speeds up our metabolism and makes it nearly impossible for us to control the beast. They used to use it at sex parties, until the males lost control and started to kill each other. It's been banned for a long time, but there is still an illegal trade off-world."

"Like Earth?" I asked.

"No. Not Earth. It doesn't affect you like it does Atlans or other planets."

"That's why I didn't go into a rage when Deek did, why I acted neurotic when he got angry."

"Exactly. We're not sure exactly why you react differently. Scientists know that some aliens—sorry, but you both qualify as aliens to Atlan's scientists—respond in different ways."

"Perhaps it's good then, that I was drugged too. Otherwise..."

I didn't finish that sentence. Didn't even want to think about it.

"You will be fine. The ReGen wand took it from your system. But for Deek, for an Atlan, even as big as he is, this drug will bring forth the beast, make him feel as if he has mating fever." Dax picked up the box and we all looked down into it at the tainted necklace. "In the other races, like yours, it makes the heart race. It brings heat and thirst and it..."

"Horny," I supplied. "It makes you horny."

"Oh, shit." Sarah put her hands on her hips. "So this drug must have been used on Deek."

I nodded. "It had to be. Deek touched it when he put the necklace on me. He went crazy right after that. So, he must have gotten enough on his skin to react." I looked up at Dax. "That means—"

"Deek doesn't have mating fever. He was drugged."

"And he's mine." Rage rolled through me at the thought of what had almost happened. "Engel drugged him. But why? I thought they were family."

Dax's frown deepened. "I believe Engel was on board

Battleship Brekk when Deek was first struck with the mating fever."

The implication was obvious, but I was so ready to scratch someone's eyes out that I couldn't help but seethe. "He's been drugging Deek from the start, trying to get him executed."

Sarah crossed her arms. "Or mated to his daughter."

I took a deep breath and tried to think. Think! "Why would Engel do this? They're family, right? What does he have to gain? Even if Deek had mated Tia, I don't get it. It's not like that much would have changed."

Dax put the box down and paced the kitchen, his anger making his eyes darken. I recognized the signs of the beast rising in response to his rage, and quickly stepped out of the way as Sarah rushed to his side to calm him.

"Let's all settle down, call the guard, and go over to Engel's house and ask, shall we? We have time."

I did a quick calculation. "Five and a half hours."

Dax's shoulders were a bit larger than they'd been moments ago, but he allowed Sarah to run her hand up and down his back, help him maintain control. "Councilor Engel is a very powerful man. When Deek turned him in for illegal arms dealing to a non-member planet, he was free in a matter of hours."

"What?" Sarah gasped and I was right there with her. "What arms deals? What the hell are you talking about?"

Dax braced his hands on the island countertop in the center of the room and stared at the necklace as he spoke. "Deek told me about it in his office the other day, when you two were visiting."

"Told you what?" I asked, stepping closer.

"Engel was on board the *Brekk*, overseeing a special shipment of food and medical supplies to a war-torn planet called Xerima. They are a primitive people, scavengers and barbarians who still fight like ancient warlords over territory and females. They are smart, fierce fighters, and are very good at stealing technology from other races."

"So? What does this have to do with Deek?" Oh, I really, really wanted to strangle Engel now.

"Deek caught him hiding top-grade ion blasters and sonar cannons in the medical supplies. Xerima is protected by the Coalition Fleet, but they are not a full member planet. Giving them arms, transport technology or ships is expressly forbidden by the Interstellar Coalition."

Sarah's breath left her body in a long, slow hiss. "So, Deek caught him and turned him in."

"Yes. But Engel was freed within hours and never faced an inquiry." Dax looked disgusted. "He has friends in very high places."

God, did this political bullshit have to be everywhere? I thought Earth politics were bad. "So? So what? He drugged my mate and was going to let him die. He has to pay."

Dax nodded. "I agree. But we're going to need proof. We need to get the guards involved now, before we try to take him down."

Sarah and I looked at each other. She shrugged. "Okay. So call them or whatever. We've got the necklace."

Dax shook his head. "I know. But Deek had several crates loaded with weapons as proof and it wasn't enough. Engel's going to have to confess, and we've got to trick him into doing it."

As he raised his gaze to mine, I saw worry there. "You'll have to get him to admit it, Tiffani. If we can get a recording of him admitting what he's done, we'll release it to the news monitors for planet-wide broadcast. He won't be able to bury it, like he's done everything else."

Shit. Confessions were not my area of specialty. I was a waitress, not a cop. Still, I'd do whatever it took to save Deek. "I want Deek home and Engel dead."

"Amen to that," Sarah added.

I looked at Dax and squared my shoulders. "Just tell me what to do."

Seranda and her big tits could just go fuck some other big Atlan warrior. Deek was mine, and I was going to get him out of that fucking prison. Right after I helped Dax kill the asshole who put him there. Well, maybe not kill him, but I was going to kick him in the nuts so hard he wouldn't be able to use his junk for at least a month. And then I'd let Dax have him. Based on the rage practically shimmering all around Dax's body, I wouldn't have to worry about justice for my mate.

And I was very, very grateful that Deek had such loyal friends. "Thanks, guys. I won't forget this. Ever."

Sarah reached over and took my hand. "We Earth girls gotta stick together."

I nodded, both relief and hope forming tears in my eyes.

Sarah squeezed. "Let's go gut that asshole and get your man."

Dax led us over to the table where we all sat like generals planning an upcoming battle. "All right, here's the plan..."

13

I TOOK a deep breath to settle my nerves. Everyone said it felt like butterflies, but for me, it felt more like a heart attack. My palms were sweaty, my heart was beating frantically and it was almost impossible to remain calm. But the plan required me to be super chill, so when the vid screen connected with Tia, across town in her father's house, I pasted on a brilliant smile.

"Tiffani!" Tia said, sitting down in a chair in front of her screen. "Are you all right?"

Her gaze raked over me—or what she could see of me through the screen.

"It took me a few minutes to figure out this stupid machine to call you, but yeah, I'm fine. Great, in fact."

She frowned.

"You look really... excited."

"Yes," I replied, for once thrilled that I was antsy. It came across as excited. I *was* excited that we'd found the reason for Deek's rage and that Dax had sent men to the jail to stall the execution, if needed.

Getting Engel to confess was all that was needed to save him and it was my job to do so.

"I am really excited. You're not going to believe the news."

"What is it?" she asked. "Is it about Deek?"

I nodded and a tear slipped down my cheek. That wasn't fake and I was overcome knowing he really was my mate.

"Let me get my father. He'll want to hear the good news. Let me just get him."

I watched as she rose from the chair. She no longer wore the dress from the party but the usual dress worn by Atlan women, hers in a pale pink.

"Father!" she called from a distance, as if she were calling to the far reaches of their house.

Deek had said he lived in a mansion. As a councilor, he was wealthy. I stared at the walls of an empty room, and the posh furnishings, the artwork on the walls, confirmed it.

Tia returned and settled into the chair. Engel came to stand behind her, his hand on her shoulder.

"All right, you've kept me in suspense long enough," Tia said, her eyes wide and eager. "What is it?"

"It's Deek. He doesn't have the fever. He was drugged."

Tia frowned while I thought I saw a tightening of Engel's knuckles on her shoulder.

"Drugged?"

I nodded. "Yes, can you imagine? One of the guards at the jail recognized the symptoms and tested him. I guess it was something called Rush." I waved my hand in the air.

"God, I'm just a waitress from Earth so I don't know about these things, but I guess he touched something that was laced with it."

"Are you kidding me?" Tia asked, clearly appalled. She looked up at her father.

"I know, I can't believe it!" I smiled brightly and looked at Engel. He didn't even blink.

"That's... incredible," he said. "But he had the fever more than once. How is it possible?"

I shook my head, played dumb. "I have no idea. Like I said, I'd heard of Rush before now. I know he had a bout of fever that had Dax putting him through the matching process for the Bride Program. Tia, you remember how it had saved Dax, don't you?"

She nodded emphatically. "Oh, yes, everyone knows that story. They are the perfect match."

"And Dax wanted to see if he could save his friend in the same way. That's how I ended up here."

Tia was listening avidly and Engel remained stoic, but I had no doubt he was absorbing it all, thinking.

"From what Dax said, I guess it was too long ago to be able to trace the drug to anyone on the *Brekk*, or any time after that. But I guess there are guards at Dax's house, testing everything for the drug."

I ran my hand over my face as if to seem like I was wiping away any weariness, then moved my hand down to my neck, placed it over the necklace. Engel's eyes dropped to it.

"They feel confident they will find the source of the contamination and will be able to trace it back to the culprit." I shivered. "God, can you imagine who would want to do this to Deek?"

Tia shook her head in sympathy. "You're right. This is horrible."

"Deek is still in jail?"

I nodded. "He's out of a cell, but in a containment room. They've used one of those ReGen wand things on him—God, those are so cool!—but want to ensure he's fully recovered before coming home to me." I looked over my shoulder. "You can see I'm back in Deek's house, alone but safe. As for Deek, he's well guarded, so no one can harm him. That eases my mind. I should be able to get some sleep, finally."

I wondered if I sounded like a flaky Earth girl blathering away, because I had to hope Engel saw the necklace, knew it was the evidence that could put him away.

"I've seen vids of people on Rush. Scary," Tia said.

"I know. I guess those from Earth aren't bothered by it." I shrugged my shoulders. "Who knows? All I know is I'm exhausted from worry, not hyped up on drugs. I'm going to crash as soon as I get off this vid thing. I just wanted to tell you both since you're family now."

I patted the necklace again, for effect.

Tia smiled. "I'm so glad to hear this. Get a good night's rest and we will come by tomorrow to visit with both of you and share in the celebration."

"Another celebration!" I exclaimed. "But maybe you can wait until the following day? I want to do a little celebrating with Deek... alone."

I winked at her. She blushed, but winked back.

"The following day then."

I waved at the screen as Tia reached toward the display and pressed a button that ended the call. The screen went black and I dropped my hand, and my smile.

I exhaled, then spun my chair about. "Think that worked?" I asked.

Dax and Sarah stepped into the room. One of the head guards joined them.

"He'll come for the necklace. Soon, before Deek returns," the guard said. He had no emotional connection to this, but he was no less angry with it. "Once Deek is here, he won't let you out of his sight and any attempt to retrieve the necklace will fail. Engel knows that."

"Now you go to bed and wait," Dax said, his mouth grim. He'd fought the Hive for years but was bothered by evil happening on Atlan. By Atlans.

"As bait," I added.

Deek

I AWOKE to one of the military physicians waving a ReGen wand over me. Gods, I kept falling asleep. Why did I keep waking up to crazy shit? First it was Tiffani seducing me—which looking back, I didn't mind at all—then Seranda, and now this.

"Leave me the fuck alone," I growled.

"I'm sorry, Commander," he replied. "We need to assess you."

"Before execution?" I asked, swiping the wand away.

"For Rush."

My hand stilled. "Rush?"

Why the fuck did he have to test me for Rush? I lay there and let the Atlan do his work.

"As expected. You have enough Rush in your bloodstream to take out a Zoran."

"The three-legged predator from Sector 3?"

He nodded as he continued to pass the wand over me. "The readings show seven times the amount an addict pumps into his veins. Give me thirty seconds to neutralize it."

The wand's color changed from orange to blue. I'd been injured enough times to know to lie still and let the wand do its job.

The doctor put the wand away and moved away from the bed. I stood, shook my head and assessed how I felt. "Holy fuck, Doc. What is going on?" I asked.

"You were drugged."

I gave him one of my commanding looks that had the newbies quaking in their boots. The doctor didn't even blink. "From our intel, it appears someone has been drugging you with Rush to make it seem as if your mating fever has overridden your mental faculties."

I took a deep breath, then another, enjoying the feel of... nothing. For the first time in a fucking long time I felt normal. "You mean someone wanted it to make it appear as if my mating fever was uncontrollable."

He nodded. "Yes, and to have you executed."

"You mean premeditated murder. Who?"

The doctor held up his hands. "I am part of the medical unit, not the guards. It was recommended I test you for Rush. You can thank your mate for that. She is a very clever woman. You are a lucky man."

"What do you mean? My mate asked you to test me for Rush? She's from Earth. How would she even know of its existence?" Rush had been outlawed more than twenty years ago. Its use was so rare, no one bothered to test for it any longer. Use of the drug on a fellow Atlan was the lowest of low, so without honor that most warriors never even considered the possibility. "Who gave it to me?"

"I do not know, Commander. You will need to ask your mate, or Warlord Dax. But you are now free of the drug and no longer in my care."

Yes, he healed people. He didn't arrest them.

"If you proceed down the corridor, the head guard will be waiting for you. I am told that two of Warlord Dax's personal guards are waiting to escort you home."

The grav-wall was down, so I stepped into the corridor. "Doc?"

He followed, paused when I did. "Yes?"

"What if it wasn't Rush? What if it really had been the fever?"

The Atlan pursed his lips. "Then I would have signed your execution order."

I nodded once, then took off down the hall. Whoever did this to me was going to pay. Now I just had to find out what the fuck was going on.

"Guard!" I called, ready to hunt my enemy.

When I reached the end of the corridor, I saw two warriors wearing the colors of Dax's house and felt my body relax, but not much. As I approached, the older of the two men stepped forward, saluted. He looked about my age, and carried himself, and his weapon, as if he knew how to fight.

"Commander. My name is Rygor." He angled his head toward the other man. "This is Westar. Warlord Dax sent us to accompany you from your cell."

I assessed the warriors with my experienced eye. They

were both my size, and fully dressed in battle armor, but Rygor's intense gaze reeked of impatience, rage even.

"Why isn't Dax here? And where is my mate?"

The guards looked at each other, then at me, but could barely hold my gaze. It was as if they expected an outburst from me. Well, if they didn't start fucking answering my questions, that was what they would get. I crossed my arms over my chest and glared at them in the way that had new recruits pissing themselves.

Rygor cleared his throat. Instead of replying, he handed me a warrior's tote. I opened it to see a full set of armor and a weapon.

"What the hell is going on, Rygor? Start talking. Now." I wasn't wearing much; I'd stripped the dress shirt off at the doctor's request, and the pants and soft slippers on my feet were party attire. What Rygor gave me made me feel as if we were heading into battle. Familiar territory.

"Your mate had a reaction to the drug as well. Warlord Dax and Sarah were with her. When she was tested, they discovered the presence of Rush in her system."

I paused in the middle of pulling on the armor, eyed the senior guard. "Is my mate safe? Was she harmed?" The beast threatened to break through as I waited for his answer.

"Be calm, Commander. She is well." He cleared his throat again and his gaze met Westar's, briefly, before darting back to me. "At least, she was when we left your home."

I pulled the armor on over my chest, quickly settling everything in place. I felt at home in the warrior gear. It was bulky, but familiar. Comfortable even, and it helped me get into the proper mindset for what lay ahead. If Dax was delivering my armor to me, I was headed into a mission. I had to assume it involved my mate, so I was primed to kill. This time, it wasn't the Hive that was the enemy.

"What the fuck does that mean, '*she was*'? And why is she not under Warlord Dax's protection?"

Westar finally broke his silence as he handed me a small ion blaster. "She wouldn't allow it, Commander."

A growl erupted and I felt my face tighten, my eyes begin to change as the beast rushed forward. I would protect Tiffani from all danger, even if it came from herself. I held him back, barely, but my voice had changed as well. My words were a deep rumble. "Explain. Now."

Rygor handed me a pair of boots. "Put these on. We'll tell you everything on the way. The longer this takes, the longer it'll be before you can ask her yourself."

I had to agree with the man.

Westar snorted. "It will all be over by then."

I slammed first one foot, then the other into the boots. "What will be over?"

Rygor bowed slightly. "Your mate is confronting your enemy, Commander. She is under guard, but she insisted on meeting him alone."

"My mate is confronting the enemy alone?" My question echoed off the corridor walls.

I was going to spank her ass until she couldn't sit for a week. "Who the fuck is she confronting? Who drugged me?"

Rygor took off at a brisk pace, Westar and I falling in behind him with ease. By his steady rhythm and pacing, the way he stood up to my angry beast, I knew he'd been on the front lines, seen the enemy and survived. A warrior in the Coalition Fleet. I wondered why he did not have a mate of his own, why he would continue to serve Warlord Dax when he could have his own home, a mate to tame him.

"I'm afraid to tell you, sir, but it was your cousin."

My steps slowed, but didn't stop. "I don't believe you. Tia would never fucking betray me."

Westar shook his head, our booted feet making a steady, pounding beat as we hurried down the corridors. "Not Tia, her father. Engel Steen."

Rygor looked back over his shoulder, worry in his eyes. "*Councilor* Steen."

Those two words made my blood run cold. With a body free of Rush, with my mind finally clear, it made complete sense. And that made me run even faster.

My mate was out there, taking on one of the most powerful people on my planet, a man so well connected, so formidable, that two full crates of illegal weapons hadn't been enough to earn him the most basic punishment. Not even a hearing.

Engel Steen was untouchable, and my stubborn, courageous little mate was trying to take him down.

Alone.

14

ENGEL STEEN WAS AN ASS. A pompous, self-righteous, misogynistic, narcissistic—the list went on and on—ass. He would fit in perfectly on Earth. Hadn't males like him been the reason why I'd left Earth in the first place?

"Tiffani, my dear, I am so very pleased to hear of your good fortune. I am sure you are eager for the commander to return home to you." He lifted the delicate cup to his lips and beamed at me like I was his favorite fucking daughter, the brightest star on the planet, the luckiest, happiest girl around.

If I hadn't known the truth, I would have believed every fucking word. The guy deserved an Academy Award. Keeping revulsion from my face would earn me one of my own.

"Thank you, Councilor."

"Please, dear, we're family. Call me cousin, or Engel." He reached for my hand, placing his giant, gnarled one over my wrist as I was about to pour him more wine. He wore gloves, which made me want to scream at him to take them off so I could rub the tainted necklace all over him.

Little did he know, the one he kept eyeing about my neck wasn't the same one, but a replica. The real one was in a box in Warlord Dax's private safe. The remnants of Rush still on it. The evidence of his scheme out of his reach.

He squeezed me gently, as if offering comfort. The whole Atlan no touching rule, apparently, didn't apply to him. Knowing all the other rules he'd broken, I doubted he respected anyone or anything.

I smiled, and hoped he simply didn't know Earth girls well enough to read the disgust and hatred boiling just beneath the surface. "You honor me, cousin." I changed the smile from what I hoped was welcoming to wistful and lifted my hand to the treasure he was truly after. "As you did with this generous gift. Thank you again. I know Deek will be pleased to hear about your concern. I am very flattered that you stopped by to check on me, but I assure you, I am fine."

"Yes, dear. But you are family, and I couldn't bear the thought of you all alone in this giant fortress waiting for him to return." He lifted his palm from my wrist and reached for the necklace. Scumbag. "May I look at it? Would you mind? I'd like to hold it. With the commander coming home soon, I find I am feeling sentimental."

Jackpot.

"Of course." Lifting my hands to my neck, I quickly found the clasp and handed it to him, coiling the length in his open, gloved palm.

"Thank you, dear." He leaned over the gold and graphite links, inspecting them and stroking each link in turn with his fingertips, as if rubbing something onto each and every piece.

And then it dawned on me, he didn't have to steal the necklace to get rid of the evidence; he simply had to neutralize the drug. Once it was gone, there would have been no way for us to prove anything.

He took his sweet time pretending to study it and I smiled all the while, sipping my wine and watching him until he paused with a frown and looked up at me.

"This is not the necklace I gave you, dearest cousin. Where is the other one?"

"It's not?" I made my eyes as wide as humanly possible and leaned forward to look at the necklace. "I haven't taken it off since you gave it to me. I haven't even changed my clothes."

I looked down at my party dress, now rumpled and ruined. As soon as Engel was behind bars, I was burning the thing. It had been so pretty when I first put it on, but now, now it reminded me of how much evil there was in the world. No, in the universe.

"How can you tell?"

"No, it is not the same." He tried to smile at me, but I could finally see the strain around his eyes, the malice breaking through his façade. "The clasp is different. My grandmother's necklace had her initials carved into the clasp."

"Oh, no!" I put my hand to my chest in mock surprise and smirked at him as I took a sip of my wine. "What magical chemical cocktail is in your gloves? Whatever will you do if you can't destroy the evidence? Now everyone will know that you drugged your own cousin with Rush, that you are manufacturing the most hated drug on Atlan and selling it like candy."

I set my wine down on the table and pulled a blaster Dax had let me borrow—and shown me how to fire, just in case—from the side of my chair, pointing it at his chest. "Poor big, bad councilor man, outwitted by a stupid, fat Earth girl. How *humiliating*."

His eyes narrowed as he took me in, his gaze going from the blaster resting in my hand to the open hatred in my eyes.

"What do you think you're going to do with that, Tiffani?"

"I'm just the stupid Earth girl, right? What am I going to do? Shoot you."

I waved the blaster at him to emphasize my words and let a few tears slide down my cheeks, part for show and partly because I was so furious with this man that my rage needed an outlet. I actually *wanted* to kill him, and that made me even angrier. Back home, I felt guilty killing a spider. I'd catch the damn things in a cup and take them outside.

This guy had made me hate, truly hate, and I let him see it in my eyes.

"But now, *cousin*, I think I should kill you for poisoning him with Rush. He almost died because of you. It only seems fair that you should face the same end."

I swallowed, then licked my lips. When had they gone numb?

Engel smiled at me then, leaning back in his chair and crossing his arms across his chest. "Die? Today? No, dear, I'm afraid that's not quite what I had in mind."

The room started spinning and I squinted at him.

"What...?" The thought stopped, half formed as my vision got hazy. I felt the blaster fall from my lax grip. Soon, my body slumped, hitting the side of the chair in which I sat.

My eyes were open, but my vision was blurry, like trying to see underwater without goggles. Everything was fuzzy and distorted.

I knew Engel rose from his seat and placed his palm under my chin, lifting my face to look up at him.

"As you said yourself, *stupid Earth girl*. Did you really think you could outwit me?" He peeled the gloves off his hands and stuffed them in his pocket. "The gloves weren't coated with an antidote for Rush, sweet cousin."

He lifted the necklace and placed it back around my neck, the brush of his fingers sending an icy chill down my spine. But my horror never showed on the surface. I was like a mannequin. I felt completely detached. Emotionless. I knew, if I really wanted to, I could talk. I could blink. I could spit in his face, but I didn't have the energy and the rest of my body was dead weight.

"The necklace really was for you, dear." His grip on my chin turned painful, and still I could not move. It was as if my entire body was paralyzed from the neck down. "And now, you will tell me where the real one is."

"Go fuck yourself." The words were quiet and slurred, but he couldn't miss hearing them.

He lifted me from the chair as if I were a feather, his hands around my throat. "Where is the necklace?"

I struggled to breathe, but I couldn't fight him, couldn't grab his hand and tug it away. "You poisoned Deek," I coughed out.

He laughed, and the sound was pure evil.

I wanted to scratch his eyes out, but I couldn't. "I hate you."

"I don't need your love, Tiffani." His gaze raked up and down my body with blatant male interest. "Perhaps I will fuck you before I kill you, see what magic your pussy has that could save an Atlan beast from an overdose of Rush."

I couldn't even shake my head. "No."

"Deek may have survived this time, but I can have him sent to the front lines again, to a Hive mission where he'll be captured and turned. Yes, that's a fate worse than death, isn't it?" He tossed me onto the floor like a rag doll and I could not defend myself, could not even tuck my head and roll. I gazed at the mating cuffs on his wrists, wondered, if his mate was dead, how he had held on for so long. Had the cuffs kept him sane? Even if his mate was dead?

"Deek will kill you."

"Perhaps. But you'll die first."

Luckily, my body was mostly numb, but my head hit the hard marble floor and felt like an exploding melon.

A roar sounded from somewhere nearby. Opening my eyes was like shoving hot metal pokers into my mind, the light an explosion of pain. But I knew that roar. I knew that Atlan. That beast. And they were both mine.

Deek

RYGOR AND WESTAR escorted me to the back entrance of my home and we sneaked inside like burglars. They'd filled me in on the way, covering everything I'd been missing. The more I heard, the more my beast started to take over. I knew Tiffani was confronting Engel, trying to force a confession from him. I knew she was being monitored by both Atlan guards and Warlord Dax.

It wasn't enough. My beast raged and my eyes remained a constant black as I fought to wrestle him down. Tiffani didn't need my beast in a blind, killing rage. She needed me to think.

Which was fucking impossible when the only thing my beast could envision was Engel touching her, hurting her.

I rushed up the back stairwell to a room where Warlord Dax and three armed members of the Atlan guard watched my mate and Engel on a system of monitors. I knew they were recording every word, but I couldn't hear any of it.

I watched as Tiffani smiled and sipped her wine, as if she hadn't a care in the world. Seeing her safe and whole helped calm my beast's protective rage and I silently nudged Dax, forcing him to hand over his earpiece. I wanted to hear every fucking word.

Logic demanded that I let her finish what she'd started. If I interfered now, Engel would walk away to threaten us again and again. As long as he was alive and free, he was a lethal threat. As much as I hated this, Tiffani was right about that. We had to stop him, and we would need a confession to do it, something he couldn't cover up. But if that asshole even looked like he was thinking about threatening my mate, I was going to rip him in half with my bare hands.

I scowled, stepping closer to the monitors as I heard Engel's voice first. He held my great-grandmother's necklace in his hands. Tiffani must have taken it off and handed it to him.

"No, it is not the same. The clasp is different. My grandmother's necklace had her initials carved into the clasp."

"Oh, no!" Tiffani put her hand on her chest and leaned back. *"What magical chemical cocktail is in your gloves? Whatever will you do if you can't destroy the evidence? Now everyone will know that you drugged your own cousin with Rush, that you are manufacturing the most hated drug on Atlan and selling it like candy."*

She set down her wine and my heart began to pound. What the fuck was she doing, taunting a cold-blooded killer like that? The room in which they sat was too far away. It would take me at least ten seconds at full speed to reach her. He could kill her by then.

Her voice poked and prodded him some more, and as much as I wanted to run to her side, I had to admire her courage. She was the bravest, most beautiful mate. And she was doing it all for me. Getting Engel to admit his crimes was the only way for me to be completely and irrevocably exonerated, and for us to live out the rest of our lives in peace.

"Poor big, bad councilor man, outwitted by a stupid, fat Earth girl. How humiliating."

Tiffani pulled a blaster and I turned to Dax, who nodded and whispered, "Don't worry, Deek. She knows how to use it."

"What the fuck were you thinking, giving her a blaster?" I demanded. I didn't want a weapon anywhere near her, even if it was in her own hands.

"You'd rather have her in there with him unarmed?" Dax shrugged. "She wasn't supposed to pull it on him. It was supposed to be a last resort."

"Fuck."

Engel spoke and I returned my attention to the screen. *"What do you think you're going to do with that, Tiffani?"*

"I'm just the stupid Earth girl, right? What am I going to do? Shoot you."

I watched tears slide down Tiffani's beautiful face. She was in pain. For me.

And then she threatened to kill him.

My heart froze, stone-cold ice flooding my veins. I didn't fucking care if she killed him, he deserved to die. But she'd just threatened a warlord, a battle-hardened warrior who'd survived more than a decade in the Hive wars.

If she was going to kill him, she better fucking do it and stop talking.

I rushed for the door but Dax and one of the guards held me back. "Not yet, Deek. He's about to confess. Don't take this away from her."

"He'll fucking kill her." My beast growled and I grew taller, my teeth aching as they burst forward, my gums retracting to reveal the razor-sharp edges.

Engel's smug voice caused me to turn back to the monitors. I realized I had nearly rushed from the room with the earpiece still in my ears. *"Not quite what I had in mind."*

"What...?" Tiffani sounded confused. Weak. I watched her go slack, her body slipping from her control and a low rumbling growl filled the room.

"Stupid Earth girl. Did you really think you could outwit me?" He peeled the gloves off his hands and stuffed them in his pocket. *"The gloves weren't coated with an antidote for Rush, sweet cousin."*

Poison. He'd fucking poisoned my mate. Right before my eyes. And Dax's. And the guards.

"Fuck," I growled.

Dax hissed and the guard on my left tightened his grip. "Don't move, Commander. We need to know what he gave her."

Engel put her necklace back around her neck and I had to turn away, unable to bear the sight of him touching her. *"The necklace really was for you, dear. And now, you will tell me where the real one is."*

"Go fuck yourself."

15

 eek

THERE WAS MY BEAUTIFUL, stubborn mate. Pride filled me at her open defiance, her courage, even as I fought to let her finish this, to make sure Engel had no options, no way out. I had to honor her courage, her desire to help, but I didn't have to like it. Then rage took over. It took all of Dax's strength and two guards to hold me back as Engel's voice grew more demanding.

"Where is the necklace?"

"You poisoned Deek."

There was nothing sane in his laughter. I raised my gaze to the monitor to find my mate dangling from his huge hands, hands that were wrapped around her soft throat.

And the beast broke free.

I barreled down the hallway and into the room where Engel stood over my mate. The growl from my beast shook the walls. It had been crazed when the Rush had hit my system. I'd been enraged when the Hive had hurt my warriors. I'd even been infuriated when I'd learned from Seranda that Tiffani had left me. But this, seeing Tiffani on the floor, under the influence of another fucking drug, indefensible and weak, was when my beast erupted. As an Atlan, I had no control over it, nor did I want any. I wanted it to rip Engel limb from limb. I wanted to destroy him.

Nothing was going to get in my way. Not Dax, not the guards. Nothing.

In my periphery, I saw Dax by the doorway with the others, waiting. He would step in, but not now. Now it was time for me to end this once and for all.

It was me and my beast against the danger to my mate.

He was going to die.

"It does not appear you have recovered from the fever, Commander," Engel taunted me, especially since he remained calm, unaffected by my beast.

"You die." Two words, and even that was an effort. My beast simply wanted to fight.

Engel circled, his own eyes turning black in response to my threat. Still, he shrugged. "Losing a mate is worse than death, isn't it? Perhaps when your cherished Tiffani is dead, you will see that perhaps *you* should have made different choices."

I stalked forward, my armor tight and my heart pounding. The beast did not charge. He was still too close to our mate. And I knew exactly what he was talking about. His drugs and guns, the shipment I'd denied him. "Xerima."

Engel placed himself between me and Tiffani, who remained limp on the floor. My beast could hear her heart beating, but it seemed sluggish. Slow. Soon, I would have no choice, I would have to charge and hope I could get to Engel before he killed her.

"What's the point of having family in high places if they can't help? It was simple, Commander. A signature was all it would have taken to prevent all of this."

He was admitting his crime. Perhaps he knew he was going to die. Perhaps he knew that everyone was aware of his crimes. He'd drugged my mate. For that alone, he'd be put away for life. The rest, it was punishable by death. Execution.

"Greed. No honor." My beast voice raged at him and I took a step closer.

Engel's eyes were completely black, his face elongating as he began to change. "I have money, you idiot. Money and power."

And that was true. He was one of the most powerful leaders on our planet. Honored. Revered. Richer even than the most decorated warlords returned from the war. So why would he deal in Rush and illegal weapons? It didn't make sense to me. "Why do this?" Three words. A complete sentence. Before Tiffani, that would have been impossible.

"I was bored, Deek. Really. I spent ten years tearing Hive soldiers limb from limb. I came home and wore slippers and sipped wine." Engel lifted his arms and waved around the rich tapestries, art and elegant furnishing of the sitting room. "This is all nothing, Deek. In time, you will see that. I had a chance to change the outcome of the war on Xerima, to influence the development of an entire civilization."

"You play god."

"We are gods, you fool. Most are simply cowards, too afraid to rule."

I shook my head, slowly, curled my beast-sized hands

into fists. He was insane. I saw it then, the maniacal belief in his gaze.

I lunged for him then. He was expecting it, let me come into his space, allowed me to grab him. The aggression fed his own beast, fueled the inner animal to rage, transforming Engel into his beast form as well. He grew to my size, his graying hair strange to my vision. Not many men of his age or stature transformed, and the sight was strange. But his body was pure muscle, his shoulders and chest equal in size to mine. He was huge, powerful, and he knew how to fight.

But I was fighting for more than my own ego. I was fighting for Tiffani.

We struggled, testing one another's raw strength. Back and forth, neither gaining the upper hand. I heard the guards arrive, but ignored them. Their blasters would simply piss me off in this form and they would do little to stop Engel. Warlords who'd fought on the front lines learned to deal with the pain of a blaster.

"No, don't intervene." I heard Dax's words, but focused on Engel. He shoved me away and we circled one another as he wiped blood from his mouth with the back of his hand. His beast was breathing hard, sweat dripped from his brow.

"Never get between warriors in beast mode. Do I have to send you back to basic training? Get a ReGen wand in here. The commander doesn't need our help, but his mate does."

Engel lunged and I deflected his punch, parried with a strike of my own to his kidney, hooked his face and pulled back and down, forcing the bastard's head up. Using my claws, I ripped across his face, twisting his neck. Unfortunately, he turned his body as I would have snapped his spine, only scarring him with deep gouges of my beast's nails horizontally across his face. Blood poured from the wounds as a howl emerged, shook the room.

Panting, I leaned forward, arms out in front, ready for more. Seeing my mark on his face, knowing that he'd go to his death with this shame upon him, had my beast howling in triumph. But we weren't done yet.

He charged me this time, his howl of rage like an explosion in the room. I used his momentum against him. Stepping to the side, I threw him down on the floor and thrust my claws into his back.

Beyond thought, I thrust through flesh to bone, wrapped my hands around his spine and twisted until I felt the bones snap, first one, then two, then more as Engel screamed in agony beneath me.

I held him there, my hand wrapped around his spine as he flailed with his arms. His legs ceased moving and my beast snarled with satisfaction. We had hurt him, ruined him, destroyed our enemy. Engel would not rise, he would not walk, he would never fight again.

And still I could not let go. He pushed up with his arms and I pushed my fist deeper, separating the bones and puncturing soft tissue. I knew his lungs filled with blood. His arms collapsed and he slumped to the floor, his body growing cold, in shock. He blinked slowly as blood dribbled from his mouth onto the floor.

The beast was finished with him. Done. Triumphant. But I would not let go, not until he'd taken his last breath.

"Deek. Deek!" I felt the hand on my shoulder, heard the voice, but it was difficult to break through the haze of hate. Of rage. Of fury. It wasn't the beast that wasn't listening, but the Atlan warrior. I wanted Engel dead. The beast, though, listened to his mate and she was talking now.

It calmed and nudged me, hard, to feel my mate's hand on my shoulder, to hear her words.

"Deek, let go. It's done," she said. She squeezed my shoulder and I tore my gaze from the paralyzed Engel to look up at Tiffani.

"It's over for him. Leave him for the guards."

"But he hurt you," I countered. I could not let this chance go by. I needed to destroy the warrior who'd harmed her.

"He did. He harmed you, too." She swallowed then, for it was a fresh wound for her. "But it's over."

"He must die," I vowed.

She nodded as she cupped my sweaty cheek, stroked her thumb just below my eye. My beast leaned into the touch and preened. "He will die, but not by your hand. Let Dax get in here and heal him."

"No!" The beast and I were in complete agreement, but Dax stepped forward, fucking ReGen wand already glowing blue and ready to help the bastard.

"Let him face the council, Deek," Dax told me. "I can't heal his spine, but he'll be healed enough for transport to jail. I promise you, he'll be executed when the council learns what he's done."

Tiffani's eyes were round, pleading. "Let them do this. Let the guards have him. I don't want him to taint you. Please."

My little mate was trying to protect me from feeling guilt. What she did not understand was that I had no remorse, no regrets. If Engel died here and now, I would never feel a moment's guilt. But her heart was soft, her worry genuine, and so I would appease her. Not because I would suffer for killing the man who'd hurt her, but because she would suffer and worry about me.

I was much colder than she knew. I was a killer. A warrior. Only for her did my heart beat. Only for her did I feel pain.

My grip was stiff as I opened my fingers and released my hold on Engel. But I did it for her.

Dax stood behind Tiffani, arms crossed, ion blaster in his hand and waited as the ReGen wand worked. Once done, he motioned with his head and the guards bent down and grabbed Engel and half carried, half dragged him from the room, the criminal's cries of pain receding.

"Thank you." Tiffani fell to her knees before me. I could feel the warmth from her skin, her scent swirling between us and I breathed it in deep. "I wanted him dead, too. I did. I should have shot him. I should have protected you."

My eyes widened. Tiffani was softness and light, love and laughter. I could not imagine such evil touching her. "Gods, no. I forbid it. You don't need that kind of evil on your hands. It blackens your soul."

"That's right." She placed her hand on my chest and I could feel my heart rate slow. Feel the way her touch had a calming affect not just on my beast, but on me.

"I can't let you have that on your hands, either. Why? Because *I'm* supposed to be taking care of you. Me. Your mate."

I took a deep breath, then another one.

"I don't ever want to see him again. Promise me, you'll see him dead?" I asked Dax, tilting my chin up to meet his eyes.

"I will. I will report to you when it's done. You see to your mate. The ReGen wand removed all effects of the paralyzing agent. She's fine."

I was thankful for my friend, for his clear thinking, for tending to my mate while I beat the shit out of Engel. But now it was time to reverse the roles. Dax would tend to Engel—I wouldn't mind if he beat the shit out of him some more—and I would take care of Tiffani.

"Well enough to spank?" I asked.

Tiffani's eyes widened and Dax chuckled. "Well enough, I assume."

"Deek, I don't think—"

"That's right, you didn't think."

I was better right then, the world righting itself, finally coming into focus. And Tiffani was at the center of it.

"Putting your life in danger like that? Calling yourself fat *and* stupid? It's time for a spanking, Tiffani."

She sputtered as I stood and picked her up into my arms. She was the perfect handful, just right. For me. I would never let her go again.

I carried her to the bedroom, dropping the cuffs she'd abandoned onto the bed before entering the bathing room. I heard Dax down below, escorting everyone out of my home. Tiffani's home. *Our* home. And no one was ever going to threaten her again.

She remained silent until we heard the front door slam shut, courtesy of Dax, no doubt. I pushed Tiffany back against the wall in the shower and turned on the warm water.

Biting her plump lower lip, her eyes filled with tears as she looked up at me. "You can't spank me! I was trying to save you."

I didn't answer her right away, simply ripped the now

wet dress from her soft body and let it drop to the floor. I washed her thoroughly, needing every ounce of this day, any hint of the drug or Engel, gone from her body.

My big hands were fast, efficient, for I didn't want to fuck her here in the shower, with Engel's blood swirling in the water at our feet. I wanted her cleansed and ready in *my* bed, mine. All mine.

Finished, I ignored the rise and fall of her chest, the darkening of her eyes, and stripped my armor, dropping it next to hers on the shower floor. I scrubbed the touch of Seranda from my body, Engel's blood and hatred flowing away with the smell of fresh soap.

I inhaled deeply, enjoying the scent of my mate's wet skin, her heat, her wet pussy.

Oh, yes, she was hot and wet, ready for me. Her gaze lingered on my chest and shoulders, my hips. When she stared at my cock, her cheeks turned pink, her breathing grew shallow.

"I'm yours, Tiffani. Every fucking inch of me."

Clean, I turned off the water as she watched me with uncertainty in her gaze. I intended to make sure she never, ever had that look in her eyes again. She was mine. And after today, she was never going to doubt it again.

I wrapped her in a towel, not bothering with drying myself, and carried her to the bedroom. "I'm going to spank you now, mate. But this spanking isn't for punishment, although Gods knows you need one."

"What other kind of spanking is there?" she asked, when I tossed her onto the bed. She bounced once, then settled. Grabbing her ankle, I flipped her onto her stomach.

I didn't waste time as I pushed the towel up until her

bare ass was exposed. The lush, creamy swells of her bottom made my beast howl and my cock harden.

She looked over her shoulder at me, her eyes narrowed. But she wasn't moving. She remained where I put her and that boded well. She liked my dominant hand, my need to reestablish control. She needed this release as much as I did.

I climbed onto the bed beside her until my knee nestled the swell of her large breast. I placed one hand on her back and the other on her ass, to pet her, stroke her, get her ready. My eyes shifted from her perfect ass to her face. "Do you need to be fucked, Tiffani?"

She bit her lip and nodded.

"Are you mine, Tiffani, my mate?"

"Yes."

"Really? Are you certain?"

She frowned. "Yes, I'm yours and you're mine."

I reached behind her and lifted her cuffs from the bedding, dangled them in front of her face. I knew my eyes darkened, for the beast did not like her bare wrists.

"Then why did you take these off?"

16

SHE SWALLOWED. "I HAD TO."

"You gave me to Seranda."

Shaking her head, she came up onto her knees so we were almost eye level. "No, of course not. Did you think I *wanted* you to fuck her?" Tears filled her eyes, but didn't fall. "Did you?"

"That's three, Tiffani."

"Three?"

"I'm counting the reasons why your ass should be spanked."

"Did you fuck her?" she asked again, her voice so unsure, so unlike the fearless woman I had grown to love.

Holding up my wrists, I let her see that my cuffs were still on. "I belong to you and no one else. But you? You say you're mine, but aren't wearing my cuffs."

They weren't required by Atlan law for us to remain mated, but I wanted the sign, the outward proof that Tiffani belonged to me. Not all Atlans needed that level of connection, but Dax and Sarah remained cuffed and inseparable. Apparently, I wasn't as independent as I'd once believed. I wanted her with me, beside me, always. I never thought I'd be the Atlan who needed his mate to wear the damn things, to tether me to her side like I was her pet, but apparently, I did. I needed that gold around her wrist not just to show the world that she was mine, but to assure the beast within that we belonged to her as well.

She grabbed them from me as if to put them back on, but I removed them from her fingers. Kissing one wrist, then the other, I locked the cuffs around her as gently as I could. The act was one of reverence, of complete devotion, and I wanted her to feel that from me. "Never take them off again, Tiffani. I beg you. My heart can't take it."

"I'm sorry, Deek. I didn't want to. But I couldn't let you die. I had to let you go. I had to give Seranda a chance to save you." Tears fell from her eyes even as darker emotions filled them. Anger. Jealousy. Pain. "No matter the cost."

Stroking her cheek—Gods, it was so silky soft—I offered her a small smile. "Yes, I know that now. But, woman, I never want to wake up to any naked female but you. Do you understand me? I'd rather die than lose you."

"I couldn't let you die."

I shut her up with a quick kiss before continuing. "I do not want you facing down Atlan warlords, criminals, or any other threat on your own."

"I wasn't on my own."

I growled then, warrior and beast.

She looked down.

"Yes, Deek."

"Now over my knees for your spanking, and then I'll give you the fucking you need."

I saw heat flare in her eyes, but she didn't move. "I don't need to be spanked."

Still on my knees, I tugged her over my lap, her head and upper body on the mattress beside me, the towel bunched beneath her waist, her ass ripe and ready atop my thighs. I tugged the towel free and tossed it on the floor. With gentle hands, I gathered her long hair and moved it to the side so I would have an unobstructed view of her plump curves, the side of her face, the need in her eyes.

Caressing the smooth skin, I said, "*I* need to spank you, to know that you are mine, to know that you are well. *You* need a spanking because you need the release. You are too strong, too brave. You hold everything inside, Tiffani. I won't allow you to hide from me, not your fear, your relief, or your desire. It's time to let everything go."

I didn't delay. My palm connected with her ass again and again, making the perfect globes tremble beneath my palm over and over, each sharp slap of my palm making her jump, tremble and gasp.

Smack!

Smack!

Smack!

I kept at it until her slow stream of tears turned into a torrent of sobs, until she stopped fighting her own emotions and let me see her, really see her.

"Don't hide from me, Tiffani. I want everything."

She shook her head, denying me, and I spanked her

again and again, not stopping until her bare bottom blushed a deep rose.

She cried out several times, but didn't move. Her eyes were closed, her face strained as tears leaked from beneath her eyelids. I spanked her twice more, then shoved one of her thighs off my lap, opening her pussy to me.

I didn't wait, the wet scent of her more than enough invitation. Moving slowly, I thrust two fingers deep, moved them in and out several times as her eyes fluttered and she whimpered beneath me.

"You had me so scared. I've never been so afraid in my life. I learned the truth about Engel from the guards and what you were doing and I almost died then and there. I swear my heart stopped."

I continued to fuck her with my fingers, telling her how out of control and desperate I'd been. I also told her how much I loved her, how I couldn't live without her. How seeing the cuffs on the floor of my cell had ripped open my heart, made my beast howl in pain.

Through my words, she learned how her actions, while they had been solely to help me, had made me age ten years.

"I couldn't just let you die," she cried. "I love you. I'd rather live without you than let you die."

I stilled my hand then, stroked the heated skin.

"I don't want an apology, Tiffani. I love that you're so brave, so fiercely protective of your mate. I just want you to understand why you're over my knee, why I'm giving you a sound spanking."

I took a deep breath.

"Because I put myself in danger?" She started to cry again then, gently at first, then deep sobs.

"No, love. Because you are hiding from me, not telling me what you are thinking, what you need." I moved my fingers again. In. Out. Slowly, so slowly. Once my fingers were buried in her pussy, I flicked a third over her clit. "What do you need?"

"You."

The beast in me had had enough of my gentleness, my games. I flipped her onto her back and locked her cuffs above her head, on the special ring attached to the wall above my bed. When she was laid out for me like a feast, I knelt between her legs and pushed her knees open wide, my gaze roaming every inch of what was mine.

Reaching down, I fitted matching locks around her ankles. She didn't fight me, didn't protest as I restrained her spread wide, locking her in place for my pleasure.

I crawled over her body, my hard cock sliding into her pussy in one solid thrust. She gasped and tilted her hips to take me deeper.

"Do you want me to fuck you, mate?"

"Yes." She squirmed. "Harder."

TIFFANI

I couldn't move. My arms were restrained above my head and my ankles had thick metal bands around each one. Deek knelt between my legs, holding me open, breathing me in like I was a feast and he a starved man.

My bottom stung, the heat spreading through me like a drug, making me tingle. The tears had come hard and fast, all my fear for Deek, my desperation, my pain at losing him, poured out of me as he spanked me. And now, now I was empty, horny, and totally his.

His eyes turned black as they raked over my body, lingering on my breasts and full stomach, the core of me that I knew was coated with welcome. I needed him inside me, riding me hard. I needed to forget about the whole damn day. I didn't want to think anymore. I just wanted to feel.

My pussy clenched as he crawled over me like a predator ready to strike. His cock was a thick surprise, going deep with one confident thrust as he caged me in with his upper body.

God, he was so big, so dominant, so perfect. I couldn't stop the gasp that escaped any more than I could deny him when he asked me if I wanted him to fuck me.

God, yes! Hard and fast and so deep I'd never get him out.

"Yes." I tried to tilt my hips, to force him to move, but he held himself still above me, his thick length spreading me open, stretching me, filling me, but not giving me what I needed. "Harder."

His eyes, which had faded back to green, turned beast black at my demand and I stared him down, challenged the monster within him and dared him to take me, to fuck me, to make me his.

With a roar, he did, transforming as he thrust in and out, hard and fast. The bed shook with his desire and I wanted to wrap my legs around his hips, tangle my hands in his hair, force him to kiss me, to fondle my breasts, to suck my hard nipple into his mouth.

Tied to the bed, trapped, I could do nothing but submit.

And that made me lose control. I stopped fighting myself, told my stupid fucking brain, my years of being rejected for my size, to shut the hell up and enjoy the ride.

He fucked me like he would never get enough, like I was the only woman who could tame him.

And I was. He was mine.

Mine.

He shifted, lifted my ass from the bed and wrapped one arm around me, beneath my hips so he could pull me up and onto his cock. He rocked my body hard and fast, my back arched, my body exposed and totally out of my control. His other hand moved to my breasts, pulling and kneading, pinching my nipples as my pussy clenched around him with each little bite of pain.

When I was thrashing, begging to come, begging him to let me come, he moved his free hand to my clit and rubbed me with firm, rapid strokes of his strong fingers. His fingers moved over me, sliding through my folds, slick with my own juices, faster, better than my favorite vibrator with fresh batteries set on high.

And still he fucked me like a machine. His pace relentless. I didn't have time to think. To breathe.

I could only scream as I came all over his cock. But he didn't stop, pushing me over again as soon as the first orgasm had rolled through me.

My mate smiled then, his face half man, half beast as he pulled his cock free from me. I felt empty, my pussy walls clenching down on nothing.

"No. Deek! No!" I was too hot, too horny, too out of control. "I need you. Fuck me. More. I need more."

"Don't worry, mate, I'm not done with you yet." His grin

was pure satisfied male as he lowered his mouth to my clit and sucked until I saw stars. I rode the edge, my pussy empty and aching as he used his mouth and tongue to tease me, to take me to the very edge of release over and over, but never let me come.

"Deek, please. Please." I couldn't take any more. I needed him inside me. Filling me. Completing me. Making me feel like we'd never be separated again. Making me whole.

"Mate." He kissed his way up my sweaty body, lingering on my breasts, sucking on each nipple until I begged him to stop, to kiss me on the lips, to fill me up with his cock.

He lowered his forearms on each side of my head and took my mouth. I moaned in welcome, tears of relief, of need leaking from my closed eyes as I gave him everything. I didn't hold back. I surrendered and kept nothing for myself.

I sighed when he filled me again, his cock moving inside me in a leisurely pace so at odds with his prior wildness that I knew something was different.

He had fucked me before. He'd fucked me dozens of times since my arrival.

But this? This was deeper. I felt like he was worshipping my body, loving me with more than words.

He kissed me with his cock buried deep, connecting us. He didn't rush, didn't demand, simply let me know that he loved me, that I was safe in his arms, sheltered beneath him, and always would be.

I tore my lips from his and stared up into the greenest eyes I'd ever seen.

"I love you, Deek."

"I love you, too, mate. Never, ever doubt that again."

I nodded and lifted my lips to his, kissing him with as much tender devotion as he'd shown me. He growled in response, and I felt his cock grow impossibly bigger inside me right before he filled me with his seed, his life, his promise of forever.

A SPECIAL THANK YOU TO MY READERS...

Want more? I've got **hidden** bonus content on my web site *exclusively* for those on my <u>mailing list.</u>

If you are already on my email list, you don't need to do a thing! Simply scroll to the bottom of my newsletter emails and click on the **super-secret** link.

Not a member? What are you waiting for? In addition to ALL of my bonus content (great new stuff will be added regularly) you will be the first to hear about my newest release the second it hits the stores—AND you will get a free book as a special welcome gift.

Sign up now! http://freescifiromance.com

FIND YOUR INTERSTELLAR MATCH!

YOUR mate is out there. Take the test today and discover your perfect match. Are you ready for a sexy alien mate (or two)?

VOLUNTEER NOW!

interstellarbridesprogram.com

DO YOU LOVE AUDIOBOOKS?

Grace Goodwin's books are now available as audiobooks...everywhere.

LET'S TALK SPOILER ROOM!

Interested in joining my **Sci-Fi Squad**? Meet new like-minded sci-fi romance fanatics and chat with Grace! Get excerpts, cover reveals and sneak peeks before anyone else. Be part of a private Facebook group that shares pictures and fun news! Join here:

https://www.facebook.com/groups/scifisquad/

***

Want to talk about Grace Goodwin books with others? Join the **SPOILER ROOM** and spoil away! Your GG BFFs are waiting! (And so is Grace)

Join here:

https://www.facebook.com/groups/ggspoilerroom/

GET A FREE BOOK!

JOIN MY MAILING LIST TO BE THE FIRST TO KNOW OF NEW
RELEASES, FREE BOOKS, SPECIAL PRICES AND OTHER
AUTHOR GIVEAWAYS.

http://freescifiromance.com

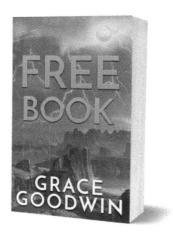

ALSO BY GRACE GOODWIN

Interstellar Brides® Program

Mastered by Her Mates

Assigned a Mate

Mated to the Warriors

Claimed by Her Mates

Taken by Her Mates

Mated to the Beast

Tamed by the Beast

Mated to the Vikens

Her Mate's Secret Baby

Mating Fever

Her Viken Mates

Fighting For Their Mate

Her Rogue Mates

Claimed By The Vikens

The Commanders' Mate

Matched and Mated

Hunted

Viken Command

The Rebel and the Rogue

Interstellar Brides® Program: The Colony

Surrender to the Cyborgs

Mated to the Cyborgs

Cyborg Seduction

Her Cyborg Beast

Cyborg Fever

Rogue Cyborg

Cyborg's Secret Baby

Her Cyborg Warriors

Interstellar Brides® Program: The Virgins

The Alien's Mate

Claiming His Virgin

His Virgin Mate

His Virgin Bride

Interstellar Brides® Program: Ascension Saga

Ascension Saga, book 1

Ascension Saga, book 2

Ascension Saga, book 3

Trinity: Ascension Saga - Volume 1

Ascension Saga, book 4

Ascension Saga, book 5

Ascension Saga, book 6

Faith: Ascension Saga - Volume 2

Ascension Saga, book 7

Ascension Saga, book 8

Ascension Saga, book 9

Destiny: Ascension Saga - Volume 3

Other Books

Their Conquered Bride

Wild Wolf Claiming: A Howl's Romance

ABOUT GRACE

Grace Goodwin is a USA Today and international best-selling author of Sci-Fi and Paranormal romance with more than one million books sold. Grace's titles are available worldwide in multiple languages in ebook, print and audio formats. Two best friends, one left-brained, the other right-brained, make up the award-winning writing duo that is Grace Goodwin.

They are both mothers, escape room enthusiasts, avid readers and intrepid defenders of their preferred beverages. (There may or may not be an ongoing tea vs. coffee war occurring during their daily communications.) Grace loves to hear from readers!

All of Grace's books can be read as sexy, stand-alone adventures. But be careful, she likes her heroes hot and her love scenes hotter. You have been warned...

www.gracegoodwin.com
gracegoodwinauthor@gmail.com

Lightning Source UK Ltd.
Milton Keynes UK
UKHW021222240221
379240UK00012B/2821